Sign up for Crystal Springs Mystery mailing list and receive *Dead Witch Talking – The Prequel*
Crystal Springs Mystery Books
crystalspringsmystery.meharmon.com

Copyright © 2019 by Paula Lester and M.E. Harmon

All rights reserved.

No portion of this book may be reproduced in any form without written permission from the publisher or author, except as permitted by U.S. copyright law.

Cover by germancreative

Chapter 1

"Nifty, nifty—life begins at fifty," Cascade Lorne sang as she brushed paint onto the wall of her entryway. The big five-oh was only a few days away. It was another birthday, but it felt like a looming, hairy beast waiting to pounce.

Fifty! How in the world did that happen?

Just yesterday, she was graduating from college and planning for her wedding. She hopped down from the step ladder and backed up a couple of steps to survey her work.

Lordy, Sterling would have hated this color. The thought of the disgusted expression on her ex-husband's face made Cas burst into a fit of giggles. The idea of him hating the entryway's new color delighted her. Boy, he would hate her plans for the rest of the house.

The freedom to make her own decisions, even about something as simple as a paint color, made Cascade bask in the bright choice even more.

Divorce. To put it simply, divorce sucked eggs.

Deep down, she still had a flicker of love for her ex-husband. Sterling had been a risk taker. He'd loved taking life by the horns and wrestling it to the ground. Once upon a time, that had been alluring and sexy to Cascade.

Before they'd met, life had been one disappointment after another for her. She'd been a scared little girl. Sterling had been the spark that had woken her up to live—to strive.

The last ten years flashed back to her in a rush. She grimaced. He had changed so radically, almost overnight. To be fair, she had evolved too. But for Sterling, it had been as if a vampire had sucked all the wonderful vividness out of him, leaving behind a bland shell of a man.

Yeah, he would hate this color, Cascade decided with a nod. Hopefully he wasn't in some casino somewhere, losing all his money. Addiction was the monster that changed her husband.

Cas turned in a circle. Every inch of boring old beige would be replaced with bright décor. If she was going to be fifty *and* single, Cas was going to start doing things her way. Determined, Cascade looked around for the second gallon of paint she'd bought. It had to be there somewhere. The loud jangle of the doorbell made Cas jump.

She opened the door to find her neighbor, Mr. Percy, standing there holding the very paint can she'd been looking for. Sitting next to him was his little dog, a West Highland White Terrier with short legs, a lolling tongue, and a sweetly wagging stub of a tail.

"Hi there, Cassie! I saw this in your driveway while I was walking Demon past your house. Thought you might need it." Smiling, he held the can out.

Cas felt a surge of annoyance at his use of the nickname she never went by. Then she groaned while eyeing the can. The game her strange neighbor liked to play was about to begin.

It was hard to tell exactly how old Percy was. He was of average height with light brown hair that had begun to creep away from his hairline. Sometimes he seemed healthy and a little on the plump side. Other times, he appeared haggard, as if he'd suddenly lost twenty pounds due to illness.

Overall, he was a nice enough fellow, always coming over and offering to do various tasks, even before Sterling moved out. But Cascade swore he always made an excuse to touch her. It was never anything overtly inappropriate but always enough to be a little unsettling.

Sterling had laughed off her concerns. So what if some people were naturally a little touchy-feely? She was being silly. As long Percy didn't cross the line, she should ignore him.

Percy continued to dangle the can in the space between them. With a sigh Cascade hoped wasn't too loud, she reached out. "Why, thank you, Mr. Percy. I was looking for that."

In the instant her palm wrapped around the metal handle, his grip shifted enough for his fingers to brush against hers. For the span of a heartbeat, they indulged in a mini tug-o-war for the paint can.

Before the moment could become truly awkward, Mr. Percy released his hostage. "No trouble at all, no trouble at all," he said with a smile wide enough to show off small but perfect white teeth. He bounced up on his toes a bit and peered over her shoulder, as if hankering for an invitation inside.

When it was clear he wasn't going to make a move to leave, Cascade decided to embrace the moment.

"Um, this is good timing." She put the can down beside the front door to keep it from closing. "I could use some fresh air and a little sunshine. The house is filled with paint fumes. C'mon, I'll stroll with you and Demon to the sidewalk."

Cas crossed over the threshold and suddenly felt as if someone had tied bags of sand to her limbs. Goodness, where had all her energy gone? She covered her mouth and yawned.

"Getting enough sleep these days?" Mr. Percy averted his eyes and developed a sudden interest in the rose bush next to Cascade's front porch.

"I thought so, but maybe not. I feel so lethargic all of a sudden." She moved past Mr. Percy, being careful not to touch him, and paused until he got the hint and fell in step next to her.

They slowed on the sidewalk in front of her house. The weather was still summer-like, but Cascade could feel the sly hint of crispness underneath the warm breeze.

Her neighborhood was a suburb that had sprouted up around Crystal Springs, a major tourist hotspot. The homes here were eclectic. Some were two-story colonials while others were one-level ranches. Cas' house was sort of in between—a cozy split level with brown bricks on the bottom and green siding on the upper story. She kept the grass in front edged, and trimmings from her mother's rose bushes had rooted and blossomed strong and healthy.

She arched her back and bent down to give Demon a scratch. The dog lavished in the attention and rolled over to put her tummy in easy reach. Cas couldn't fathom why Percy had named this sweet, fluffy little thing such a strange name. She thought Angel suited her much better.

Mr. Percy chose the same moment to pet his dog, resulting in another brushing of hands.

"Have you noticed a woman hanging around the neighborhood a lot lately, Mr. Percy?" Cas asked, drawing her hand back and taking a tiny half-step away. "I keep seeing her over and over. She has long, auburn hair, with an average build and about my height. She looks out of place somehow."

"Out of place like she's lost?"

Cassie shook her head. "No, not exactly. I guess it's just a feeling I have. Her clothes are a little dated, but I'm no fashion goddess myself." Cas laughed, but Mr. Percy's lips turned downward and his forehead creased.

Cas hurried on. "Sometimes I see her walking around the neighborhood, or every once in a while, when I'm bringing in groceries or something, I'll catch her staring right at me from across the street. She seems...sad somehow."

Mr. Percy scanned up and down the block as if the woman would appear like a specter. "If you think she's up to no good, we should call the sheriff's office and make a report."

"No, no. It's not that serious. She's probably just moved to the neighborhood or something." Actually, Cas had had the uncomfortable feeling that the woman was following or watching her. She shivered at the thought but brushed it aside. Who would want to watch her? She wasn't interesting in the slightest.

"Well, I can't say as if I've seen anyone like that. But it sure seems like people are moving in and out of our neighborhood at record speed lately," Mr. Percy said while ignoring Demon's attempt to chase a squirrel. The little dog yapped and jumped up and down at the end of her leash.

"I've noticed that too. I think it must have something to do with the new auto paint production company outside of town. It's putting Carlson's, the small paint company here, out of business. Probably some people are losing their jobs and moving on out while others are getting hired by the new place and moving in." At least that was the only logical hypothesis Cas could come up with.

"True, true. You're probably right about that. Do you need any help with your painting project?"

The abrupt change of subject jarred Cas, and she stammered a little. "Uh, n . . . no, I'll be fine. It's my entryway walls right now, so it's a small space. It's the edging that I hate most, and I'm done with that part. It sure did make me feel tired, though." She stifled another yawn and Mr. Percy's lips twitched upward a little.

It wasn't quite a smile. No, it was more of a smirk. Did she say something smirk-worthy? What an odd man. She had half a mind to ask about it when a truck rumbled around the corner.

They both turned to watch as a white Chevy Silverado pulled into the driveway of the house to the west of Cas'. "Huh. Another new person," Mr. Percy mused.

"He moved in a couple of days ago. Seems really nice, but I haven't talked to him yet or anything."

Their new neighbor had to be about 5'11—tall but not too tall for Cas' taste. Dark stubble dotted his cheeks, but he was the kind of man who made five o'clock shadow look downright sexy. He maneuvered out of the truck but went around to grab something from the passenger seat. It gave Cas a nice, long look at his rear view. The guy was slim but still managed to fill out his black t-shirt in all the right places.

In fact, she was still staring at all his assets when he turned around and waved at them.

They both waved back, but Mr. Percy made a disgruntled noise under his breath. "He looks like a pretty boy to me," he said. "One of those guys who gets by on his looks and doesn't actually know how to do any real work. He's probably an executive at that new auto paint plant. I bet he sits in a big, cushy office chair all day with his feet up, planning golf outings and sending his secretary for coffee every twenty minutes."

Wish I was his secretary, Cas thought, but aloud she said, "Why, Mr. Percy, how could you know all that from just looking at the man? He seems perfectly cheerful and kind to me." Cas was a little shocked at the vehemence in her neighbor's voice, and she allowed a mild reproachful tone to creep into her own.

Maybe he'd been bullied by guys who looked like Hottie McHotterson before. She laughed to herself about the nickname. Her new neighbor was hot, and she was single now. She found herself enjoying the feeling of being interested in a man who wasn't Sterling.

"Well, I'm a good judge of character is all. I can tell a lot about a person by how they carry themselves, and I don't think I like the new neighbor. If I were you, I'd keep him at arm's length." Mr. Percy crinkled his nose.

It was Mr. Percy who Cas wanted to keep at arm's length. She tried not to stare but couldn't help herself as Hottie opened his front door. Yeah, it would be nice to get closer to him. But would a guy like that be into a woman like her? Did men her age desire women her age?

Thanks to yoga, she was in fantastic shape. She could use a hair trim though. Her russet-brown locks were past her shoulders, way longer than Cas preferred.

Mr. Percy cleared his throat. With a small sigh and a last lingering look, she turned back to him. He was touching her *again*.

Percy patted Cas' shoulder. "I have to get going now, Cassie. Demon here needs to finish her business. You take care.

And if you change your mind about wanting help with the painting, you just call me up, and I'll come right over."

"Thank you, Mr. Percy. I will. You and Demon have a good evening."

Cas' eyes wandered to Hottie's house as she headed back toward her own front door.

Maybe she should bake something for him. A *welcome to the neighborhood* peach pie or something. Or a lasagna. Something too big for him to eat by himself. Lasagna and pie, with garlic bread and salad too. And wine. He'd have to invite her to join him, wouldn't he? He couldn't eat all that food alone. Unless he wasn't by himself. Or interested in women. Oh, please be single and straight, Hottie McHotterson!

But bringing over food would be too obvious, wouldn't it? The thought made her deflate. Cascade imagined every single woman within fifty miles stopping by with a casserole dish in hand. She couldn't just throw herself at him like that. What did women do nowadays? Text?

When she'd still been married, Cas had daydreamed about having a hot date with some gorgeous man who was totally into her. But since the divorce, she hadn't exactly jumped back into dating. She'd gone online and looked at some of the dating websites. But she didn't even have the nerve to download the current popular dating app. The idea of strange men judging her based on a stupid picture made her cringe.

She yawned again as she reached her door and pushed it open. Maybe all this stressing out about dating was making her so darn tired. Cas really was exhausted all of a sudden, but that entryway wasn't going to paint itself.

She chuckled at the idea of bringing a bottle of red to Hottie's house. That wouldn't be happening tonight but speaking of wine—she'd welcome a glass right now.

Cascade brought a glass of merlot back to the entryway. Wine was truly divine—a few sips and she was starting to get her second wind. But the drop in energy had been strange. Maybe she was coming down with something. She made a mental note to take some vitamin C before bed, just in case.

Cas hummed to herself as she poured more paint into the pan. She had just picked up the brush when the doorbell rang again. "Grand Central Station around here today." Feeling mildly irritated at a new interruption, Cas plopped the paintbrush down, wiped her hands on an old paint smock, and moved to open the door. She prayed it wasn't Percy again. One encounter per day with Mr. Touchy was more than enough.

For a moment, Cas didn't know what to make of the person standing there. The visitor was . . . well, the word that came to mind was small. Before her was an extremely short man. He couldn't be much taller than four feet high. He was also reed-thin, which compounded his overall small vibe. Cas decided that the green tinge of his skin must be a trick of the evening light. He had yellow hair—not blond, but actually yellow. And to top it all off—Cas blinked to make sure she wasn't going nuts—peculiar silver flecks within his ice-blue eyes seemed to twinkle.

The man smiled up at her. "Hello, Miss! I'm from SunSprite Deliveries. Package for you. Sign here, please."

SunSprite? What an odd name. But, if there were such a thing as sprites, he'd be a good one.

The funny little man held out a clipboard. As she signed her name at the bottom of the delivery form, another strange thought occurred to Cas. Maybe this was some type of practical joke. Perhaps taking whatever this guy offered was a bad idea.

But the package already sat heavy in her hands. The delivery man pranced—yes, the little skip-dance he did qualified as prancing—down her walkway toward his van. And the van! How did she not see that thing before! It was a bright, hot-pink monstrosity with the word SunSprite sprawled in neon green across the side.

Yep, he was positively spritely.

Cascade shielded her eyes from the evening sun with her hand, trying to get a better look at the strange delivery person and his vehicle.

Movement to one side caught her eye, and there was her gorgeous neighbor again. Either it was the prancing or the blinding splash of pink, but he'd paused while unloading something from the back of his truck. He stared at the van too. Her heart fluttered when he looked toward her, and they waved at each other again.

Despite looking as if it could be part of a crazy LSD trip, the van drove off normally enough. It didn't sprout wings and fly, as she'd half expected it to.

Retreating back into her house, Cas took a sip of wine and turned her attention toward the heavy package. It was addressed, in neat cursive letters, to Miss Cascade North.

How strange. North was her maiden name. She hadn't used that in over 25 years.

A WITCH TOO LATE

The package was a rectangular box wrapped in plain brown paper. It was easy to open, and she soon found herself gazing at a smooth, fist-sized, oval-shaped river rock with ebony glyphs etched into it.

What in the world?

She picked up the rock to get a closer look. It was warm, like a person's skin. Milliseconds later, a cacophony of sound, lights, smells, and tastes accosted her all at once. It seemed like she could hear everything: leaves rustling in the trees outside, neighbors speaking in their homes, crickets in the grass, the burning pilot light in the oven, her own heartbeat, and the heartbeats of a hundred other people.

Bright colors erupted in front of Cas' eyes, as if a million fireworks had exploded and filled her vision with a kaleidoscope of hues she never knew existed. With each passing shade, a flavor erupted in her mouth. Suddenly, blue had a taste and so did emerald green, sparkling white, ebony, magenta, lilac, and so many more.

And the scents! It was all and nothing. Fresh bread and flowers, honey baked ham and ginger-bread, sweet spices, burning rubber, sour fruits, and crushed boysenberries. It was like sensing everything she'd come across in life all at once.

It was wonderful. It was majestic. It was also agony. She couldn't make sense of any of it, didn't know where it was coming from, and behind her eyes, a small, stabbing pain grew into a very large one. Her legs felt like useless blubber attached to a torso filled with water.

Was this what death felt like?

She felt herself falling. She heard the smack as her head hit the floor.

The last thought she had before a sweeping cloak of blackness enveloped everything was—so much for enjoying my fifties and living my way.

Chapter 2

Cascade blinked up at Hottie McHotterson, who stood in the entryway of her home, smiling. It was like he was in a toothpaste commercial—his teeth were so bright that she almost felt like covering her eyes for a second. "I'm single, straight, and available," he said. The tiniest hint of a dimple appeared on his right cheek.

He held a hand out toward her, but as she reached to take it, he pivoted and began using a hammer to pound at her partially coral-colored walls. Bang, bang, bang!

Where had that hammer come from? Her heart thudded with alarm as she tried to understand what Hottie was doing.

Then her eyes flew open, Hottie was gone, and she stared up at the white, popcorn textured ceiling in her foyer. What in the world?

It took a minute, but Cas realized the hammering was real. Someone banged on her front door. But why had she been dreaming on the floor in the entryway in the first place?

Her mind was foggy. She strained to sit up. The last thing Cas remembered, she'd been painting and having a glass of wine. Geez, she'd only had one sip.

Cas managed to stand and rubbed at her eyes, which felt swollen, like she'd been crying for hours. She took a deep breath, finally feeling the fuzziness at the edges of her consciousness begin to recede.

The package!

She remembered it all now: SunSprite Delivery, the funny man and his pink van, and the strange package he'd given her to open. She looked around the floor for the mysterious stone but couldn't see it. Instead, pieces of a gorgeous aqua and turquoise vase she'd inherited from her mother and kept on a table in her foyer now covered the tile. Her eyes welled up with tears. She pushed them down. Cas reminded herself that the vase was a thing and not her mom.

She must have tipped it over somehow. Cascade did a quick pat-down. OK, no obvious injuries—that was good. Tomorrow, however, she'd probably be sore from the fall.

Someone still knocked on the door non-stop. Giving the floor one last pass with her eyes, wondering what could have happened to the river stone, she smoothed her hair down, and pulled the door open.

"Happy Blossom Day!" A wall of sparkles filled the air. A high-pitched, screeching horn noise shattered the air. Cas winced and covered her ears. As the glittery confetti hit the ground, Cas saw a woman on her front stoop, blowing into a noisemaker.

Cas blinked several times, wondering if she might have a concussion. Wow, this one looked stranger than the delivery guy. But the woman didn't disappear or change and now spoke excitedly.

"I'm Juniper Crossings, and I'm here to greet the new witch! Where's the lucky young person?" Juniper's curly hair stood out in all directions as though she'd touched a Tesla coil. She appeared cross-eyed, but as Cas studied her more, she realized it was an optical illusion from the ultra-thick-paned glasses she wore. The giant round, red frames clashed with Juniper's strawberry-blonde hair.

Cascade stared at the woman. Did she say greet the new witch?

Juniper peered back through the thick glasses. Her eyes fixed on Cascade's open mouth. After another second of no response, she mumbled, "Oh bother, this is going to be one of *those* houses. Okay, let's see."

"Hello!" she said, speaking louder and over-pronouncing every syllable. "I'm Juniper Crossings and I'm," she pointed at her chest, "here to greet the new witch. WHERE IS THE YOUNG PERSON?"

Cascade took a step back. "I'm not hard of hearing. I'm confused. Young person? Witch? I'm not sure what you mean. I'm the only one who lives here," she managed to sputter out.

"Only one, you say? Huh. I'm sure I have the right house. Hold on." Juniper shrugged a giant purple knapsack off her back, set it on the concrete stoop, and rifled through it, murmuring to herself all the while. She started pulling things out of the sack, one by one, and dropping them next to it.

"I followed the witch's hat, I'm sure of it. Where did I put that iPad? I know I stuffed it back in here when I arrived and fished the whistle out. Hmmm." The strange woman pulled a jump rope, a cowbell, and half of a peanut butter sandwich out of the knapsack, dropping them on the stoop. A tiny, yellow bird suddenly flew out. It fluttered over Juniper's shoulder and peered into the sack too.

Despite the weirdness of the situation, Cascade couldn't help but smile and think for a second about how wonderful it would be to have a pet. Maybe she did have a concussion.

"I can't imagine how I could have gotten it wrong. Oh, here it is!" Juniper triumphantly held a small iPad up over her head. "Okay, let's have a look at this together, shall we?"

Cas couldn't help herself—she stepped out onto the stoop for a better look. The sun had set, and the violet and purple shades of twilight filled the sky. The street was quiet. For half a second, the thought crossed her mind that maybe she was still lying in the foyer, knocked out and dreaming. Cas pushed the thought aside. As strange as it was, she was wide awake, and this was happening. A crazy-looking, absent-minded but so far harmless stranger stood on her stoop, talking about witches and flashing an iPad.

Well, she'd been hoping for a later-in-life adventure, so she shouldn't look a gift horse in the mouth, right? Her mom used to say that all the time, before she died. Cas had never understood it until she was older.

Maybe this woman had the wrong address. She could be one of those entertainers who did themed witch or wizard kid parties.

But what kid's party would be this late?

Cas studied Juniper's iPad, which showed a map of her neighborhood at the street level. The wild-haired woman touched the screen and it zoomed in on Cas' green house with a black witch's hat hovering over it.

"See?" Juniper sounded pleased with herself. "It's your house that's been marked. Someone in it has blossomed, for sure! There are no mistakes in this program; the developers made it with iron-clad magic. You're positive you don't have an adolescent in there?" She peered through her glasses at Cascade and stretched to peer into the house. A crease appeared in the middle of Juniper's forehead as she strained to see inside. She looked back at Cas and raised one eyebrow.

"No. It's only me," Cas said. "I'm a divorcee who never had kids."

"Well, you can't be the newspring. You're too old. Uh... I mean... that is to say... witches blossom at puberty, usually. And you're, well—past puberty." Juniper trailed off, giving Cas a small, apologetic smile.

"I'm way past puberty," Cas confirmed with a chuckle, and Juniper looked relieved. "Now, what's all this about blossoming and newsprings and witches?"

"I'm Juniper..."

"Crossings. Yes, I got that. But who are you? Who do you represent? Why are you at my house with an iPad and confetti and a whistle, talking about witches?" Cas always believed in being polite. But a person could only abide so much nonsense before getting rude.

"I work for the Department of Newspring Wellbeing and Services. When a new witch comes into his or her powers, we're notified, and I go to their house to greet them, offer an official welcome to the magical community, answer any questions they might have, and make sure the family knows about all the current resources available to them. But I'm sure you know all of this."

Witches, huh? Department of Newspring Services? Cas had to give the woman credit. Her delusion was very thorough.

A burst of adrenaline suddenly shot through Cas, causing her heart to beat faster and a slight tingling feeling in her whole body. She'd wished for some excitement and here it was, in the form of Juniper Crossings, right on her own front stoop. She could either turn away and go back to her painting or embrace whatever madness this unexpected visitor might be bringing into her life. It didn't take her long to decide.

She was going back to her painting.

Excitement was one thing. Jumping head first into full-out craziness was another. Cas looked Juniper over. The other woman appeared odd, and at the moment, rooted to her doorstep. It seemed smart to entertain her a bit, keep things pleasant, and send this Juniper person on her way.

"Um, a witch? No. In fact, I don't really have much of a family," Cas answered. "So, you must have me confused with someone else. Sorry about that, but now I have to go. Wait—I probably shouldn't ask this—"

"You may ask me anything. That's my job."

"Yeah, thanks for that." Cas debated the wisdom of asking a silly question but decided to indulge anyway. "Why did you think I should know all of this?"

Juniper started and gestured at Cas from head to toe. "Dear, I can practically smell the power coming off you. You're a witch, of course. Probably from a long line of them with juice like that. But that doesn't explain why my newspring locator would be off." She shook the iPad and slapped it a few times. "It must be going hinky. Now, they told me how to reboot this silly thing..."

Juniper stabbed and poked, flipped the device over, then poked and prodded some more. When she pulled a screwdriver out of the backpack, Cas decided to step in.

"Here, let me. I have one of these." She leaned over and pressed one of the buttons until the screen went dark. "It will take a few minutes to boot back up."

"Thank you. If it was up to me, the entire department would run on crystals and potions. But oooh nooo! My new supervisor loves techno-magic. Says it's efficient. I think it's ludicrous."

They both peered at the black screen for a few seconds before meeting each other's eyes. An awkward moment passed.

Juniper rocked on her heels. "So strange we haven't met before, you living so close to Crystal Springs. What's your house?"

"I'm sorry?"

"You know, your house of magical study. Or are you a generalist?"

Cascade shook her head slowly. "I'm not what you think I am."

"Pshaw!" Juniper chuckled. "Of course you are. Someone with your potency? Your aura is like watching a lightning storm. I have a degree in auraneisalogic studies. Not a witch! You're funny."

Juniper slapped her leg and laughed. But then she noticed Cascade.

"You're not laughing. Aren't you joking?"

"Nope."

"Have you conducted any experiments lately? Tried to brew up a new potion? Sometimes a witch will tinker with the wrong spell and their short-term memory goes bye-bye. That's what I guessed earlier when you weren't catching what I was throwing."

"I'm afraid not. No."

Juniper frowned. The iPad beeped as it turned back on. She tapped at the screen. "Impossible. This program is never wrong.

I don't understand." She glanced from the iPad to Cascade and back to the device. "Unless somehow... you...are the newspring? No. How could that be?

"Hmm. This is far outside of my normal duties. I've never cared for an adult newspring before. In fact, I've never even heard of someone blossoming at your age. Er, sorry again."

Cas waved off the woman's apology and edged backward. "Oh, don't worry about it. I know I'm almost fifty. It's not news to me. So, you believe these new witches bloom . . ."

"Blossom."

"Yes, of course. They blossom at puberty and their families care for them? Teach them how to be witches and all that?" Cas rested a hand on the door. It was time to end this conversation. But as she moved away, the other woman moved closer.

Juniper nodded, her curls bouncing around her head. "Precisely!"

"None of that ever happened to me. Sorry. You must have the wrong house. If you'll excuse me."

Cas started to close the door, but Juniper planted her palm against it with a loud smack.

"I want you to listen to me very closely, Cascade Lorne," Juniper said in a steady, low-pitched tone.

"How do you know my name?"

"It's in my locator program but forget that. Did anything out of the ordinary happen to you today? Anything?"

The change in the woman's voice made Cas pause. This conversation was going from strange and whimsical to plain strange. It was getting dark, and there still wasn't a neighbor in sight. She locked a firm grip on the door and glanced at Juniper's hand.

"It's been nice chatting, but I have to go now."

"This is important." Juniper followed Cas' gaze and dropped her hand away. "I apologize for seeming peculiar. But dear, this is vital. Did anything strange happen today or even earlier this week?"

Cas shook her head and started to shut the door. "Sorry I couldn't be of help, but you have a good night."

Juniper didn't respond. She made a twisting motion with her fingers.

Cas saw the movement and gave the door a quick shove. It moved an inch and refused to budge further.

"Was that a yes or no? Anything odd happen?" Small, tight lines appeared around the edges of Juniper's mouth.

No matter what she did, the front door wouldn't close. Cas pushed at it, yanked the doorknob, and wiggled it back and forth. She gave up with a snort and squinted at Juniper, exasperated. "Yes, something odd did happen right before you came."

The other woman gave a small, encouraging nod for her to continue.

How could she get rid of this Juniper woman when the front door wouldn't shut? Cas rubbed her forehead and relented. "Somebody sent me a rock." She turned around, hoping to spot the stone nearby. But it wasn't anywhere in sight.

"It's not here anymore. What could have happened to it?" She searched the foyer, even grabbing a stir-stick and submerging it into paint can to feel whether the stone had fallen into it.

To Cas' chagrin, Juniper and the bird followed her inside the house.

"A rock?" Juniper asked, looking even more bewildered than her normal resting face appeared.

"Someone delivered a package to me before you came. I opened it, and there was a rock inside, covered with strange writing—like hieroglyphics but different. I touched it and I must have blacked out, knocking over my vase." Another twinge of regret shot through her at that thought, but she pushed it away again and continued. "I woke up when you banged on the door. But the rock isn't here now."

Juniper clucked her tongue and her brow furrowed again. "A stone with writing on it? Without it here, I have no way of telling if it was cursed or not."

"Cursed! What are talking about? There's no such thing as cursed objects." Cas threw her hands up, frustrated with the conversation. The tiny yellow bird performed loops around her head.

"This seems to be out of your league. And frankly, this is out of my wheelhouse too. A witch who thinks she isn't a witch. I've never!" Juniper tapped an index finger against her lower lip. Suddenly, Juniper nodded once and her facial features smoothed out.

"I'll take you to the High Court. They can figure out what to do with you."

"High Court? What's that?" Cas caught herself. What was she doing? "Never mind. This has gone too far. You should leave now before I call the cops."

"Don't be silly. The police you're talking about are for humans. The High Court, however, is the governing body for all witches in this division. It's comprised of five sirens, and they handle things like this. They have an office building in Crystal Springs," Juniper answered matter-of-factly, positioning them in the middle of the room.

"That's it!" Cass shifted and grabbed the woman by the elbow. "We're done. You and your little bird have to go." Without warning, she hiccupped.

A tiny storm cloud, complete with a flash of lightening, appeared over Juniper's head. Thunder clapped and rain poured down in sheets on her and the yellow bird.

Juniper glared at Cas as she wiped rain water out of her hair. "This is magic. Your magic. You, Cascade Lorne, are a witch."

Cas stared at the rain cloud, mouth agape. No. How?

She dipped a hand under the cloud. Warm droplets splashed against her fingers. "I don't understand."

"Yes, you definitely need the High Court. You have zero control over your power. Who knows what you could do? They'll help to sort this mess out. Well, here we go then."

Juniper made a flicking gesture with her wrists and fingers, and suddenly, they were both inside something.

Cascade jumped about six inches in the air, and when she landed, the surface under her feet wasn't her living room's carpet. It was like she was inside a transparent, rubber bubble. There were several plush armchairs in the center. But the stench! It was like fourteen bodybuilders had worked out in the thing and left their body odor behind to fester. The smell almost had a physical presence, making the air heavy and a little cloudy.

Cas turned on her heel to stare wide-eyed at Juniper.

But the other woman busied herself settling into a blue velour armchair. She buckled a seat belt.

"Strap in. The ride might be a little choppy."

Before Cascade could move an inch, Juniper moved her hand again and the bubble structure began to spin. At first, the view of her living room rotated in a slow circle. There was a sudden pop, and then nothing.

The living room—her whole house—was gone.

There was no turning back now, even if she wanted to.

Chapter 3

Cas lost her footing as the bubble spun faster. She crashed into a chair and fumbled to get the seat belt buckled. She remembered what her former dance teacher had said about doing spins: focus on one spot to keep from getting dizzy.

Streaks of vibrant color covered everything outside the bubble. Silver, greens, and shades of gold passed by with increasing intensity. Instead of looking outside, she focused on Juniper. The other woman sat with her eyes closed.

Once the dizziness was under control, the next thing that demanded Cas' attention was the horrible smell. She choked on it, coughing until her eyes watered.

The sound of fireworks erupted inside the bubble contraption. Juniper's eyes popped open.

Cas jumped, and the seat belt dug into her neck. "What was that?" Her voice sounded a little hysterical. She didn't like that, but things were happening so fast.

"It was you." Juniper snapped, sounding annoyed and worried. She tapped thin fingers against the plush armrest. "You coughed, and magic erupted out of you. You're making random things happen. Try not to cough. Or hiccup. Or sneeze. Just sit there quietly. Here, this will help with the smell." She handed Cas a contraption that looked like a clothespin with soft orange pom-poms on the pinching end. "It's a nose pincher," she responded to Cas' bewildered look. "Coursers are stinky inside. It's just the way it is. We use these to deal with it."

"So this bubble thing is called a courser? What's making it move?" The nose pincher helped with the odor, but Cas had never liked being forced to breathe out of her mouth. It made her feel like she was drowning.

"Ley lines. They're invisible currents that flow between magical places. Crystal Springs is such a place. The coursers ride on the ley lines, and they're faster than cars. But a lot stinkier."

Cas' heart pounded much too fast. It was almost painful. She pulled in a lungful of air, hoping to slow it down. But the silly nose-pinchers made breathing difficult. Now it felt like the round walls of the courser were squeezing in.

She knew the bout of claustrophobia was all in her head. Cas chose to do what she always did when upset or nervous. Get information. Like her mom had always said *knowledge is power*. And right now, Cas could use some power. Everything was—literally and figuratively—spinning out of her control.

"Crystal Springs," she said. "I've always loved that town. It's so lovely. My ex-husband and I used to like to visit the hot springs. I was never much of a skier, but I enjoyed drinking wine in the lodge while other people were on the slopes."

"The town is a magical hub. There are only a large handful of them in the world: places where the elements of air, fire, water, earth, and magic converge."

"Elements?" Cas fought to keep her mind off the suffocating feel of the nose pinchers. Plus, her stomach felt queasy. Cas groaned. The spinning, though it had slowed down some now, and the nose pinchers were not a good combination.

"The mountain provides a conduit to the earth and air elements of nature, the hot springs hold open a portal to the fire element, and the Crystal River, which dumps into Sapphire Lake, is a connection with the powerful water element. All that was required was a High Court to establish a link with the element of spirit and voila! We have a magical hub. Its energy draws all manner of magical and supernatural beings to it."

Cascade had lived in this area her whole life and had never seen anything that would make her think the supernatural was real. Until today. And she still wasn't convinced this was happening. Maybe the fall had put her into a coma. Perhaps she was actually in a hospital bed, hooked up to tubes and machines keeping her alive. Her neurons could be firing off an elaborate hallucination while her body lay motionless.

Or maybe it had been a stroke. All the noise, lights, and smells she'd experienced right before she collapsed might have been her brain circuits shorting out. But she'd just been to the doctor. The doc had pronounced Cas perfectly healthy, with good cholesterol levels. Besides, there was no history of stroke in her family that she knew of.

No, this wasn't some bizarre medical mishap. Maybe this courser thing was some kind of strange government technology? Perhaps she was being kidnapped by a secret government organization that would run experiments on her.

"Why haven't I seen any witches or anything like that if Crystal Springs is such a draw for the supernatural?" she asked Juniper, speaking just above a whisper in an attempt to avoid making the nausea worse.

"Regular humans usually shy away when they feel magic," Juniper replied. "They prefer not to see and hear what they don't understand—it's easier for them than expanding their minds would be. The poor dears. But Crystal Springs is so lovely and has such wonderful attractions that the non-magical folk can't help but be drawn in for short periods. And that's a good thing. Many of us in town depend on the tourist income. But only a few actually live in the town proper."

As the Blossom Greeter spoke, Cas hiccupped without warning.

Juniper's glasses floated off the bridge of her nose as if they were pulled by invisible strings. She snatched the red specs out of the air and settled them back into place with a huff.

"Sorry," Cas murmured. "I get the hiccups under stress."

The wild-haired woman offered an amicable tsk-tsk. She reached over and patted Cas' hand.

"No. I'm sorry, dear. This is a lot for you to take in, and you're handling it very well. Not many people could deal with all that you have this afternoon without shrieking or passing out."

"I did pass out. Just a little. But I'm okay now. No more unconsciousness for me. I'm still not entirely sure what's going on, but thank you for your kindness." Cas felt a twinge in her throat and a sting behind her eyes that told her she might cry. She squeezed her eyes shut and thought about irises. They were her favorite flower.

This was a trick she'd learned in yoga class years ago. When she was upset or feeling like she might cry but didn't want to, she'd pull a picture of a dark purple iris into her mind and focus on it as hard as she could. She'd try to see its velvety petals, including a droplet of water, observe its thick yellow pollen, and watch it sway gracefully in the breeze. It did the trick every time, helping Cas feel calm and in control again.

As she focused on the flower behind her eyelids, Cas did, indeed, begin to feel calmer. The pounding in her chest slowed. And her hands stopped shaking as the adrenaline drained out of her blood stream.

In fact, the imagery was more real than it had ever been before. The smell of the iris was strong, and her fingers reflexively closed around the flower's stem.

Cas' eyes flew open and saw a deep purple iris in her hand. She squawked and tossed it away with a jerk. Her heart beat just as fast as it had before she'd tried the meditation. "Where did that come from?" she cried.

"I told you—you're powerful. You might as well add *try not to think about anything too hard* to the list of things you should avoid doing right now. Oh, look! We're here. Thank goodness. You can leave your nose pincher here. The next folks who use the courser will definitely need it."

Juniper unbuckled her seat belt and stood. Cas tried to follow suit, but her fingers shook. With a good amount of mental effort, she managed to get the belt undone. Her legs were like rubber bands, unsteady and unsure. Cas saw the flower on the floor. She thought about bending over to pick it up but felt the attempt unwise.

Juniper twisted her wrist and fingers in a complex manner. The bubble contraption suddenly snapped out of sight as though it had never been there. Cas, Juniper, and the flower dropped about six inches onto a marble floor. It was so abrupt Cas inhaled sharply and then hiccupped.

The iris burst in a pop of bright colors.

Maybe there was something to this magic thing after all? Four hours ago, she'd been painting her entryway and now rain-clouds, flowers, and fireworks exploded out of nowhere. Whenever Juniper gave a flick of the wrist, something happened. Cas stared at her hands and flipped them over. They didn't appear any different. And she didn't have to move them like Juniper for odd things to happen.

If this was all a hallucination, she'd eventually wake up. Right? Cas wasn't sure. She didn't know what to do. Play along? Would that make all this worse or better? Another hiccup burst out, and Cas slapped a hand over her mouth. It was as though a screenwriter had been put in charge of her life and composed the most bizarre scenes she could think of.

"This way!" Juniper snapped. The purple backpack bounced as she power walked away in an unsuccessful attempt to outrun another rain-cloud that had appeared.

Oops, she hadn't seen that new cloud. At least for now, the decision had been made for Cas. She followed Juniper.

The hall was unlike anything Cas had seen before. It had to stretch about the length of a football field. Grey stonework and gold-filigreed marble rose to a ceiling so high, Cas could only glimpse the highest point. It reminded her of the finest of Victorian architecture.

"Wow!" she breathed.

"This is the Courthouse," Juniper explained as Cas jogged a little to catch up with her. A few other people milled about in the big room. None of them glanced toward the two women as they moved with urgency.

The cloud had rained itself out and disappeared. Juniper led the way toward a round tile near the edge of the room.

Off-black in color, it seemed out of place next to the other square, grey tiles. "It's where the High Court works and meets. Some of them even live in apartments or penthouses here."

"It's beautiful. I had no idea there was a building like this in Crystal Springs."

"Mmhm. It's one of those things that non-magical beings tend to ignore, even though it takes up about five acres and is thirty stories high. Come along, Cascade. I need to get back to my other job. This has taken more time than it should have."

"Sorry," Cas said, following Juniper onto the round tile, even though she felt like it wasn't really her fault. She'd just been having a quiet evening at home, not intending to go out anywhere, least of all to a towering gothic structure in Crystal Springs to meet with people who thought they were some kind of witch council. This was all really Juniper's fault for showing up with her crazy stories and virtually kidnapping her.

As soon as their feet touched the round tile, Cas felt as though her body moved upward, like in an elevator, only faster. She gasped, and a tiny winged pig materialized in front of her.

It squealed, and its miniature, chubby, porcine face turned a pinkish-red. Juniper's yellow bird stuck its head out of her knapsack and squawked at the intruder. The pig flew over and they both climbed inside the sack.

Juniper sighed. "Now I have two of them to feed," she muttered.

Cas bit down on another apology, refusing to let it leave her lips. None of this was her doing.

When the moving sensation stopped, they were still standing on the round tile but hovered in midair next to a small platform. Juniper stepped off and motioned for Cas to follow.

Juniper led her down a short hallway with emerald marble floors and into a large, almost empty room. A woman sat on a high stool behind a tall desk in the middle of the otherwise empty room, filing her nails. A gold-plated sign sitting on the desk declared she was the receptionist. Despite that fact, the woman didn't look up when they entered.

"Hi, Waverly. Are the sirens in? I have a bit of an emergency," Juniper said.

The receptionist still didn't look at them. Her bright blue hair stood out in perfect two-inch spikes all over her head. The mane looked like it wouldn't move if a hurricane came by and sucked the woman inside. A matching shade of blue adorned her lips, eyes, and cheeks, and Cas wondered briefly where she'd bought her makeup. Not that she herself could ever pull off wearing a color like that. Until that moment, she wouldn't have thought that anyone could, but Waverly looked beautiful. She also had a confident air about her. It was as if Waverly knew she was stunning and felt comfortable in her own skin.

That was something Cas had been striving for throughout her whole adult life. She was fit and healthy, but she hadn't ever really found her own personal style. Her wardrobe was mostly jeans and flowy, comfy shirts.

"They're in a meeting," the blue-haired woman replied in a bored tone. "I can't disturb them. You can wait over there, and I'll let you know when they're available." She gestured toward a wall in the room against which no chairs or benches stood.

"Waverly. This is important. Please pay attention. This woman, Cascade Lorne, is forty-nine years old and just blossomed today. She doesn't know about witches or anything else supernatural and doesn't have a family to teach her. Every time she hiccups or coughs, her magic goes nutty. I need to present her to the Court and let them figure out what to do with her. Waverly!"

The secretary looked up at Juniper and then her eyes moved to Cas, traveling down her body and up again before bouncing back over to Juniper.

"I have to go back to work, so I'm going to have to leave her here with you." Juniper sounded calmer now that she had Waverly's attention. "Will you make sure her magic doesn't go haywire and hurt anyone until the sirens can take over?"

Waverly sighed deeply and put her nail file down. She hopped down from the tall chair. "I'll take her in now, I suppose. You can go, Miss Crossings."

Cas felt a jolt of panic at the thought of Juniper leaving. The Blossom Greeter was the only person she'd had contact with since touching the river stone, and though the woman was eccentric, she had been kind. Now Cas was in a new place with strange people and didn't have a car or any money to get back home. The danger of her situation was becoming apparent. "Juniper, this is insane. Just take me home in the bubble thing and I'll be fine. I promise not to do any, um, magic or whatever." She tried to sound strong and steady, but a little catch in her voice revealed the truth—she was scared.

Juniper grabbed both of Cas' hands and squeezed them. "You'll be all right, dear. The sirens will figure everything out. You're safe here. I can't take you back without them seeing you because who knows what you might accidentally do with your power? You could hurt yourself or someone else. You don't want that, right? And I have to get to my other job before I lose it. I hope to see you again soon."

With that, Juniper spun around and walked away. The pig and the yellow bird stuck their heads out of the knapsack and waved goodbye.

Cas was not going to be abandoned in some strange place. She started to follow Juniper, intending to trail her back out of the building and then find her way home. But her nose hadn't felt right since she'd been in the stinky courser with the nose pinchers on, and now a horrible pressure was building and... she sneezed.

Orange, yellow, and green silly string burst out of her nose and mouth in a blossoming 10-foot spray that landed around her in all directions. Some of it fell back onto her. It felt wet and sticky.

As Juniper disappeared out the waiting room door, someone grabbed Cas' arm. She jerked around to see Waverly standing there. The receptionist held on with a vice-like grip that Cas couldn't hope to break.

Up close, she could see the secretary's blue eyes matched her hair and makeup. And now they stared with a hard intensity that made her squirm a little in the woman's grip. "You should come with me now, Miss Lorne. Miss Crossings is right—you're an immediate danger to everyone around you and should be kept locked up."

Chapter 4

Waverly's iron grip didn't hurt, but there was no way to escape it. Cas tried planting her feet and twisting her arm this way and that, but nothing worked.

"It's magic. You aren't going to be able to get loose." Waverly sounded as bored as ever. "Juniper was right. The Council needs to see you, so I'm going to make sure they do. If you start running willy-nilly through this building, you're going to cause more trouble for all of us. Come on." The eccentric-looking receptionist guided Cas toward a door behind the high desk.

"I'm not a witch, and I don't know what any of this is about!" Cas huffed, though she had to admit that recent happenings in her life had been pretty strange. "I want to go home." That much she could say with conviction.

"Once the sirens figure out what's going on with you, I'm sure they'll let you go home." It seemed like Waverly meant to be soothing but only managed to sound blasé.

The two women entered a short hallway lined with multiple closed doors. Waverly headed straight for one at the end, opened it, and propelled Cas through. She let go of Cas' arm as the door shut behind them.

This room had darker colors on the walls and floors than the reception area. It was decorated in muted brown and gold, and a majestic chandelier hung from the center of a tall ceiling.

There were no visible chairs. Two of the walls were covered in built-in bookshelves that didn't have any books. The other was blank except for three doors spaced at odd intervals.

"Wait here. I'll get the sirens," Waverly said before exiting through a different door. Cas spun around and tried to go back out into the reception area. But the door wouldn't budge—even though she hadn't seen Waverly do anything to it.

"Okay, that's fine. I'll talk to these siren people, explain the whole misunderstanding, and then they'll let me go home." Even though she said it out loud, Cas had trouble believing it. She wandered around the edges of the room, trying the doors. They were all locked tight.

Her hands shook. Cas balled them up and forced a rising wave of panic down. She paused in front of a large window and peered down at the street. A fair number of people milled around down there. Some of them stopped and talked to each other while others walked with purpose down the sidewalk. If Juniper was to be believed, most of those people were witches. She'd visited Crystal Springs countless times. How could most of the residents be something other than human?

Cas saw a person dressed in a hooded blue cape, and something about it triggered a memory. Her mom had told her a story and, in it, a witch wore a similar cape. It had been a very exciting story for a five-year-old, and it ended with everyone living happily ever after. She remembered feeling delighted and satisfied at the conclusion of the story. Mom had hugged her and whispered, "Most witches are good, Cassie, but some are bad. You can't trust them all, and you must make your own happy ending. All by yourself."

Cas jolted, shocked at the clarity of her mother's voice in her mind. Until that moment, she hadn't had any recollection of the story or her mother saying that. What in the world? Why would her mother talk about witches as if they were real?

She pivoted when a door opened behind her. Waverly re-entered the room ahead of five other people.

"This really isn't in our schedule, you know," an elderly man with a few wisps of white hair and a handlebar mustache said. He wore what looked like red flannel pajamas and leaned much of his weight on a knotty cane. "I was just getting ready to do my morning yoga before the day's appointments. Why shouldn't this girl have to wait for an appointment slot like the others?"

In her mind, Cas imagined this man doing yoga. He looked like he'd topple over and break a bone if he tried it.

Another of the newcomers, a woman who appeared to be in her sixties, with sharply angled features and a severe bun of strawberry blonde hair that had probably been vibrantly red decades earlier, put an arm around the elderly man's shoulders. "Albert, the girl has powers that she can't control," the woman shouted into the old man's ear. "And the Blossom Greeter from the Department of Newspring Health Services says she blossomed yesterday evening, even though she's fifty years old."

"I'm forty-nine for a couple more days," Cas interjected before realizing it was probably a bad idea to open her mouth.

The severe looking woman snapped her head toward Cas. The edges of her mouth, which were already down-turned, looked like they might dive right into her neck.

"She's fifty, you say?" Albert asked, cocking his head to the side while squinting at Cas. "No one blossoms at fifty, Lavania."

Cas almost had to bite her tongue to keep from correcting him again.

"Come over here, Ms. Lorne," Waverly said from behind her. "You can have a seat here while you answer the council members' questions.

Cas had no idea what the receptionist was talking about. The blue-haired woman stood beside one of the room's smooth walls. There were no chairs in sight. Waverly waved her hand impatiently toward herself, "Come on, come on. The council has other things to do today, you know."

Waverly raised her blue eyebrows and Cas moved over next to her. The receptionist inclined her head toward the empty wall. When Cas didn't move, the woman sighed, took her by the shoulder, spun her around, and gave her a little shove.

Cas gasped as she toppled backward, and two things happened in quick succession. A chair popped into existence out of the wall, catching Cas as she fell, and a blast of cold air pelted them both with snow.

"Ach!" Waverly threw her hands over the perfect blue spikes and sprinted across the room to stand behind the sirens.

"Well, I can see that Ms. Crossings was right on one thing, anyway," the woman with the bun, whom Albert had called Lavania, said curtly. "This woman doesn't know how to control her power. You can go now, Waverly. Thank you for getting us. You did the right thing."

The receptionist left the room and the five sirens moved to the opposite wall from where Cas now sat. They moved backward until chairs popped out of the wall for them. Each of the chairs was unique, as though they were made for the person who sat upon them. Cas glanced down at her own chair.

It was a delicate Queen Anne style with gold upholstery and embroidered burgundy flowers.

Albert sat on one that looked like a cozy, overstuffed armchair covered with tattered brown fabric. Lavania sat in a high-backed, hard chair made of weathered dark wood that seemed as severe and uncomfortable as her personality. The others, two more women and a man who looked to be of varying ages between thirty-five and sixty, had their own version to sit on too.

As everyone settled in, Cas shook snow out of her hair and held back a groan. What was she doing here? What were these people going to do with her?

As if pulled by an invisible rope, her chair jerked into motion. Cas white-knuckled the arms and held on for dear life. Her seat slid to a stop near the center of the room.

Closer to the sirens now, she noticed the younger man who'd entered with the others was pretty attractive. He looked about thirty and way too young for her, but Cas couldn't help but eye him up. He smiled when he caught her staring, and heat crept into her cheeks.

Lavania cleared her throat. "From what I've been told, what we have before us, friends, is a newspring—as ludicrous as that sounds. Supposedly, she blossomed yesterday and claims to know nothing about magic."

Albert snorted in response. "Newspring, my wrinkled behind," he said.

Lavania's serious features softened a little, and one end of her mouth jerked up as though she might snicker. She caught herself, though, and wrestled the errant muscle back into submission, frowning like she had before. Cas thought the woman probably wouldn't smile if someone gave her a million dollars and a yacht to enjoy it on.

The other three witches chuckled until Lavania leveled a wicked glare in their direction, which silenced them. "So, the duty of figuring out whether she's a freak of nature or simply a liar has fallen upon us. I personally think she's a fraud. Maybe some backwater swamp witch wanting to stir up trouble for attention. Regardless, we need to figure out who she is, whether this late blossoming nonsense is genuine, and what to do about it. Right now, the Blossom Greeter and Waverly believe she's a danger to herself and others."

Lavania looked down her long, thin nose at Cas. "Let's take a good look at you."

She leaned forward, squinted, and made a circular gesture with her right hand three times, palm facing out. For a long moment, the witch seemed to study the air between herself and Cas.

The air between Lavania and Cas took on a translucent sheen, sort of like a drop of baby oil in water. The effect was like a shimmering in mid-air. But without warning, it felt as if a hundred tiny eyes hovered over every inch of Cas' skin. She squirmed under the intense scrutiny. Without thinking, she poked at the glimmer.

A loud pop made everyone in the room jump.

Lavania gasped and lurched from her seat. "How dare you interfere with the Archsiren's spell?" She pointed at Cas and snarled. "You better hope you're not a fraud, newspring. Witches who tamper with my spells regret it."

Cas shook her head in confusion. "Uh—I'm sorry. It felt kind of creepy."

Albert quipped, "Some of Lavania's spellwork does tend to have that effect."

Lavania whirled to stare at Albert, but the older man waved her down. "Easy, Lavania, no one likes to be peeped on. The girl is right."

"I was gauging her magical prowess, not peeping. It's interesting how selective your hearing is, Albert. And she," Lavania jabbed a black lacquered nail in Cascade's direction, "is far from being a girl. That's why all of this is likely a hoax meant to make the Court look bad."

He shrugged with a hint of a sly grin. "You're the Archsiren, but I've been on the court the longest. In all my years, I've rarely come across a witch who exudes power like this one." Albert gestured with his cane. "And she had the oomph to burst your spell with her pinky finger. Let's hear what she has to say."

The others nodded their agreement. A woman with sparkling bracelets climbing up both arms said, "We've all experienced it by now—her powers are quite considerable. Let's hear the newcomer out."

Lavania lips settled into a hard line. She reclaimed her seat. "Very well. What's your name?"

Cas bit her lip. A weird sort of numbness had begun to settle in her limbs. It must've been the last few hours taking their toll. Her eyes traveled over each of the sirens. None of their stares were as cold and threatening as Lavania's. Maybe it was because the woman had called her a fraud, or maybe it was the nasty look on her face, but Cas' patience was at an end.

"I'm the one who was brought here virtually against my will, has been detained *definitely* against my will, and is being questioned like a disobedient child. I think I deserve to know who all of you are before I start giving any answers." She did her best to sit up straight and folded her arms.

Silence settled over the chamber for a long moment. No one spoke as Cas sat defiant. Lavania stared down her nose as if Cas was nothing more than a gnat that needed swatting. One of the other women started to speak, but Lavania shushed her.

"Very well," Lavania raised one eyebrow slightly and gave a small, impertinent nod. "You have been brought before the High Court. I am Lavania, Archsiren and leader. Beside me sit sirens Albert, Valencia, Stu, and Shiloh."

The woman with the bracelets smiled and waved. "Shiloh Newberry. Pleasure to meet you." Her chair looked like a giant silver S that had fallen on its back.

"Shiloh, please. It's too early for all that good-naturedness," Lavania said, rubbing her temple. "We are the most powerful witches in this district, and it's our job to handle disputes, requests, and problems in the magical world within our jurisdiction. And you, my dear, seem to be a pretty big problem."

Cascade broke her defiant stare-off with Lavania. "I'm Cascade Lorne."

"How could someone not blossom until they were fifty?" Valencia glanced at Cascade. "I'm sorry—forty-nine. I've never heard of someone not blossoming during puberty. It's peculiar."

The others, besides Lavania, all nodded and verified they'd never encountered such a thing either. They spoke among themselves as if Cas wasn't there.

To her relief, the mini-snow storm had ceased, but damp hair clung to her forehead. Cas sniffled. She had a funny feeling in her nose, like being tickled by a feather. She kept trying to rub it away, but it was persistent. Perhaps she was allergic to someone's perfume?

As the sirens ignored her, Cas couldn't help but sneak glances at the younger guy. Lavania had called him Stu. He had wavy blond hair, a square chin, and full, kissable lips. She scolded herself. Now wasn't the time to check out a man, even if he was handsome. Just then, the tickly sensation got the best of her. "Oh no, not again," she said and clamped a hand over her mouth.

Cas sneezed. A stream of tiny, glittery, red papers billowed out from her ears. They floated around her head in a scarlet cloud. She looked up in wonder. At first, Cas couldn't make out what the things were. It slowly dawned on her. They were hearts. Red construction paper cut-out hearts covered in red and silver sparkles. Just like the kind she used to make in grade school.

"Oh no," she groaned and swiped at the glittery cloud. The hearts fell in a heap onto her lap and the floor around her shoes.

All the witches except Lavania erupted into laughter. Cas felt hot as blood rushed to her cheeks.

"Well, now, that's just darling," Valencia said. She wore a close-fitted, ivy green, full-length dress. Her chair was more like a small throne. A magnificent sunburst made of gold sat on top of the backrest. It circled Valencia's head like a halo. "A witch with no control who manifests her innermost emotions for everyone to see. Looks like someone has a crush." She elbowed Stu, who sat beside her. They both burst into a new round of laughter.

Lavania clapped her hands. "Valencia, Stu, enough! We need to focus. I know this seems entertaining, but it could be truly dangerous." She leaned back in her chair. "Perhaps we should kill her and be done with it."

Cas' heart smacked against her ribs. Did the woman say kill her? Could they really do that? She cast a forlorn look at the door behind her.

"No, no." Shiloh rubbed her hands together. "There's a mystery afoot. Lavania, may I?"

"Oh, go ahead." Lavania crossed her legs. "But I think my solution is the best. Are the executioners on duty today?"

"Let's not be hasty. Ms. Lorne, let's puzzle this out. Do you descend from witches, or are there any supernatural threads in your lineage?"

"No." Cas shook her head and looked at the hearts still pooled around her feet. The edges of a few had started to flake into dust. The hearts, the silly string, and the pig. It didn't make sense unless what Juniper and the others told her was true. "I didn't know magic was a real thing until weird things started happening to me."

"Hmm." Shiloh tapped her lip with a finger. "Okay, and when did these things start?"

So much had happened, Cas had to consider. "Umm...let's see. Yesterday was a strange day. But all the super weird stuff started after Juniper showed up."

"What's that? The weird stuff."

"Fireworks coming out of nowhere and going off, silly string when I sneeze ..." Cas glanced down at the few remaining hearts that hadn't dissolved yet. No need to mention those since they'd all seen it happen. "Oh, and the little flying pig."

"She made a pig fly!" Lavania's stern features hardly budged as she laughed out loud. The other sirens chuckled but not as heartily as the Archsiren.

Shiloh ignored them. "Pay no attention to them, dear. Newspring powers are unpredictable. Though the ability to manifest by mere thought is," she paused to hunt for the right word, "atypical if not slightly troubling."

"It's downright aberrant, if you ask me," Lavania growled.

Valencia wagged a finger. "I've heard stories about newspring supremes having that type of power."

"She's no supreme," Stu volunteered. "Naturally gifted—I'll give her that. But nothing more." His chair was black leather and steel. Its legs jutted out like a four-limbed spider.

Cascade frowned. They couldn't be talking about girl groups from the sixties. "What's a supreme?"

Shiloh said, "It is a witch born with an incredible connection to the source that all witches derive their magic from. For some, the connection flows like a stream or a river. For a supreme, his or her connection is like a tsunami that never stops."

"I agree with Stu. This person is no supreme." Lavania smirked at Cas.

"I don't know." Shiloh looked at the other witches. "She even has a traditional witch name."

"Humans call their offspring by nature-based names sometimes. That means nothing," Valencia said. "Besides, look at what Stu's mother named him."

Stu shrugged. "I was the eighteenth child; my mother was tired of choosing names. What can I say?"

"Stu and his mother come from a long line of witches." Shiloh turned back to Cas. "How else was it a strange day?"

"Well, for starters, an odd man delivered a package. It was addressed to me but in my maiden name."

"Tell me about him."

Cas put her hand out about waist-high. "He was this tall, with yellow hair—not blond, but yellow like a crayon. The name on his crazy pink delivery van was," she tilted her head to one side, trying to picture the vehicle and the writing on the side, "um, Sun something. Bright, Light—"

"Sprite? SunSprite?"

Cas nodded. When she did, the other witches, who had been slouching in their chairs or picking at invisible dust on their clothing, or in Albert's case, starting to doze off, came to attention. They sat up straight, listening. Even Lavania now perched straight-faced and quiet.

Shiloh scooted to the edge of her silver chair. "I see. Now we're getting somewhere. And the package?"

"Oh, it was just a rock." But even as Cas said it, she suspected it was more than that. "It was a river stone covered in black writing that looked kinda like Egyptian hieroglyphics. And when I touched it, there was a rush of...I don't know how to explain it. It was like colors, sounds, and tastes all jumbled into one. I passed out, but I chalked that up to paint fumes. I woke up to Juniper banging on my door."

Silence followed for several heartbeats.

Stu exhaled a gust of air and cursed. "Do you know what this means?"

Whatever it meant, Cas didn't hear because the witches broke out into a loud round of arguing. Some words did make their way to her. Snatches of words like rare, danger, and toxic. Impossible. Death. Forbidden.

Finally, Lavania raised a hand. "Quiet! We can debate later. Action is required now."

"It was the river stone, then," Cas said, searching their faces. "What was it?"

"It may," Lavania lips pinched so tightly they turned pale, "have been a cursed object. And you, my dear, may have been hexed."

All the twittering and chatting in the room stopped. Dead silence hung in the air after the word hexed was spoken.

"Now, we need to launch an investigation. If this is true, we can't have a forbidden magical object lying about. And there's you, Ms. Lorne. I still think you're an aberrant human. If so, there's little chance you'll be able to control your power."

Shiloh said, "She may be an aberrant, but we should check her family history, Lavania, just in case. Maybe her magical lineage has been lost over time. It can happen."

"If you insist." Lavania snapped her fingers, and a bell on a rope descended from the ceiling. She rang the bell, and a few moments later, one of the doors opened, and a man entered the room.

"Dustin, we need to know about this woman's lineage," Lavania said as she gestured. The newly arrived man's eyes followed the Archsiren's motion and landed on Cas. He smiled at her, and she couldn't help but smile back. He looked like he was about her age and had a kind air about him. She felt drawn to him—like he was on her side. Cas exhaled a tentative breath in relief. Someone acting in her best interest was a small gift.

"She may have been hexed," Lavania continued.

"That shouldn't contaminate the search, I don't think," Dustin said as he approached Cas. Out of everyone in the room, he was dressed the most casually. The most normal, Cascade thought. He wore a navy-blue blazer over a pristine white tee and matching blue slacks. It was like he was prepped for a casual Friday at the office.

"No need to stand," he said as he reached her. "This will take just a sec." He removed a long, slim piece of wood from his inside jacket pocket.

Cascade stared at it. "Is that a real wand?" It was the first thing that seemed to fit with all the talk about witches.

He smiled and whispered, "Yes, I'm a little old school, though this one has some perks." To Cascade, it appeared to be a solid piece of wood bigger than a small stick. But as she watched, Dustin peeled away one side and unfurled the wand.

Dustin leaned over to show Cascade what he held. It looked like a weathered, leather, hard-cover book. Except, in the well-worn center was the darkened indentation of a hand. Cas counted six fingers.

She looked the question up at him.

"This is a TOC—a table of contents. All members of a magical family share similar markers, sort of like DNA. This will take a sample of yours and determine any matches. And, uh, the extra finger slot, ignore that. It used to be very common once upon a time, but we mostly don't like to talk about it now." Dustin winked, and laugh lines appeared around both brown eyes. "Pop your hand right here, love. This won't hurt a bit."

A WITCH TOO LATE 49

His voice was firm yet reassuring. Cas wanted to trust him. But it wasn't as if she had much of a choice. She put her hand on the impression. And…

…nothing. Nothing happened. No sharp needle prick. No beep. No magical voice. Nothing.

"There!" Lavania shouted. "I told you all. An aberrant!"

Dustin flapped the TOC like it was fan. "Hold on. She gets cranky in the morning. One more time, if you please."

Since it didn't hurt the first time, Cas felt more confident about touching the TOC again.

Once more, nothing happened at first. The edges of the TOC shivered as if waking up. Cascade felt her face was a bit too close to the thing. She pushed back in her chair.

Dustin, however, seemed nonplussed. "There we go, old girl."

The TOC's edges flapped against Dustin's hand. It rose until it hovered a foot above his palm.

Cas stared, open-mouthed. "What is it going to do?"

"Direct me to the right book, of course."

The TOC's edges moved faster and faster until Cas couldn't make them out anymore. It flew over her head and toward one of the walls. But it was not graceful. The TOC's flight was haphazard and lopsided—it dipped and bobbed. To Cas, it looked a lot like a drunk hummingbird.

As if to prove her point, the TOC smacked into a wall, bounced off, and plopped to the floor. It curled back up with a wet-sounding rattle.

Lavania tsked. "That was pathetic. Rejuvenate the animation spell on that immediately, Dustin."

"Yes, Archsiren," Dustin answered as he retrieved the wand and tucked it away in his jacket. He reached toward the empty wall. He pulled a giant book out of nothingness. A shelf popped out of the blank wall in front of Dustin, and he set the book on it. He pulled out a pair of glasses from an inside jacket pocket and placed them on the end of his nose before opening the large tome.

"Cas," Shiloh said, "where is the river stone now?"

She forced herself to look away from Dustin. "It was gone when I woke up this morning. It must be in my house somewhere."

Cas didn't know exactly what being hexed entailed, but she didn't like it nor the way the court seemed nervous about it. Despite that, maybe now that she'd provided this piece of the puzzle, they could figure out what was going on and fix it. She just wanted to go home and get back to normal.

"Her lineage comes through her mother," Dustin announced. He'd been rifling through the book and now pointed at a line of tiny print mid-way down the page. "She died when Ms. Lorne was about five, but she was a witch."

Cas blurted out, "What?"

Feeling astonished, she moved toward Dustin, intending to look at the book, but Lavania's sharp voice stopped Cas as effectively as a leash. "Sit down, Ms. Lorne."

Cas didn't have the energy to resist. Her mother, a witch? How could that be? She found herself doing as the Archsiren bid. Did her mother keep this secret from her or had she died before being able to tell her? Dustin shot Cas a small smile. Her eyes were filling with tears, so she couldn't see his face well, but she appreciated the sentiment.

"What was the mother's name?" Lavania's voice sounded strained, as if she fought to stay in control.

Dustin adjusted his reading glasses. "Let's see. It was Oceane. Oceane Lovebrooke. Cascade's birth father is noted as human."

Lavania paled. She remained very still for some time and then asked, "Is it true? You're Oceane's child?"

Cas gave a small nod. "Yes. She was my mother."

"Hoorah, she's a born witch." Shiloh clapped her hands. "How delightful."

"Yes, delightful," Lavania mocked her fellow siren. She breathed out. "That doesn't change the matter at hand. She's a danger to herself and others. We have a responsibility to protect the community." Lavania tapped a long fingernail on the arm of her high-backed wooden chair, her eyes slightly unfocused and fixed on a spot on the wall over Cas' head. "What should we do with you now?"

"We should kill her," Albert croaked, and Cas jumped in her chair. The sound of fireworks erupted, echoing off the walls in the room and causing everyone to put their hands over their ears.

When the sound stopped, Albert said, "See? She's dangerous. Now that we've heard the woman out, killing her is the only thing to do."

"I don't think we need to kill her," Stu said. "We can banish her to Sitegard with the other magical criminals."

Cas' eyes widened at the thought of being taken somewhere remote and left to fend for herself. That wasn't going to happen. She didn't know how, but she'd fight them, magical witches or not.

She was about to stand up and flee when Dustin spoke calmly. "May I offer a suggestion? Humbly, of course, as I am certainly not a siren." He removed his glasses and waited for Lavania to nod her consent to continue before he went on. "We could take her to a relative of hers for safe-keeping. A witch who could keep her contained, perhaps teach some basic skills. Just until you can figure out what's happened and what needs to be done next. She has a half-sister named Tallulah North. She's a witch. Maybe Ms. Lorne could be taken to her. She lives right here in Crystal Springs."

Shiloh shot a hand up into the air. "I second that emotion!"

The shocks kept coming, giving Cascade no time to recover before another one hit. They knew about Tallulah? She hadn't heard from her half-sister in at least thirty-five years. How could these people possibly know about her?

"It's motion, Shiloh. How many times do I have to explain that to you?" Lavania's face hardened as she reached a decision. "Yes. We'll send her to the half-sister, Dustin. Send a peacekeeper squad to Ms. Lorne's house to find this so-called river stone. Though I warn you, Ms. Lorne, if you prove to be lying, the punishment will be swift and severe."

A buzz sounded in the room, and Lavania snapped at the air, "What is it, Waverly?"

The blue-haired receptionist's voice came into the room as though through a speaker but without any static or distance to it. "Dzovag Livings is here. He's getting impatient in the waiting room. He says his appointment was thirty minutes ago, and he's beginning to feel slighted by the Council, which isn't treating his request with the proper gravity." Waverly sounded like she was reciting this information. Her tone held its usual flat boredom.

Lavania sighed. "Yes, yes. We'll get to Mr. Livings shortly." The buzz sounded again, and Cas guessed that meant the speaker had been turned off.

Lavania turned to the others. "Well, we can't keep Mr. Livings waiting, can we? I suppose he isn't rich enough yet; he needs approval for his latest scheme so he can overcharge more humans and witches alike." Lavania stood up. "I need a cup of javabrew before I can deal with him though. Dustin, I leave Ms. Lorne with you. See to it that she makes it to Ms. North's house this morning. If she harms anyone, I'll have your head."

Cas turned toward Dustin, who walked her way with a smile and an outstretched hand. As she thought about seeing her horrible, long-avoided half-sister, she had the fleeting thought that Dustin looked like the sweet lamb who would lead her to the wolves.

Chapter 5

"She isn't answering her phone or the magical summons I sent." Dustin's lips pursed, and he tapped a pen on his leg.

"I haven't seen Tallulah in a good long while, but she was not a person inclined to bending to someone else's schedule when we were kids," Cas offered.

"A little selfish, eh?" The clerk grinned at her. He was handsome, but Cas could see he was probably older than she'd thought at first. He had a spray of fine wrinkles, and black hair with a heavy sprinkling of ivory.

"Well, I don't like labeling people, but that's how I remember her, yes. I haven't seen her since I was about thirteen years old or so. Our mom passed away when I was five and she was three, and my step-father, Tallulah's dad, didn't know what to do with us once we got to be teenagers, I guess. Next thing I knew, she was going to live with our aunt and I was in boarding school."

Cas paused. She hadn't thought about that time in a while, but now the confusion and hurt she'd felt returned. She continued in a softer voice. "I never understood why she got to stay with family and I was sent away. I felt like Cinderella, not being treated fairly by my step-father. Tallulah and I didn't keep in touch after that, really."

Cas' foot bounced as she sat on the edge of the chair. She and Dustin had moved from the council chambers to a small suite down the hall. She'd gone to the bathroom and splashed water on her face, and now she tried to keep her nervous energy from popping out in some goofy magical way.

"Hmm. Well, I guess there's nothing we can do other than have you escorted to your sister's house." Dustin smacked his hand down on the desk as if declaring the matter closed.

"Half-sister," Cas corrected. "Taken by whom?" She half hoped he would say Juniper. Even though the Blossom-greeter had really thrown Cas into a big mess and been annoying—at least Juniper was familiar in a sea of unknown.

"I'm not sure. I can't do it. I have to be available for the council all day. They often need something from me during their hearings and meetings." Dustin's lips pursed again. Cas was starting to recognize this as a sign of the clerk trying to solve a problem.

"I'll take her."

Cas jumped at the sound of the deep voice, which seemed to come from nowhere. She didn't see another person in the room and hadn't expected it. Was it coming through a magical speaker like Waverly's voice had back in the council chambers? Was someone watching them?

Cas looked around the room wildly, peering up at the ceiling. Dustin rolled back from the desk and peeked underneath. "Echo. How charitable of you. I'm surprised you would volunteer to go into one of Crystal Springs' wealthier neighborhoods. I didn't think you liked those sorts of people."

Cas leaned forward in her chair, trying to see who could fit under Dustin's desk, but the shadows were too deep.

"I don't, but I'm getting bored hanging out around here. Besides the occasional mouse to chase, there's little to occupy my mind."

A small black paw emerged from under the desk, stretching as far as it could before stepping onto the carpet. A second paw and foreleg emerged, followed by a cat's head and body. The back legs came out last, stretching out behind the small black cat as he yawned. He took several steps out from under the desk toward Cas before sitting down and cocking his head at her. His whiskers twitched a little. "Yes, I'll take her. Maybe her sister has a nice girl cat I can chat with for a while."

"Half-sister," Cas said automatically, and then she shook her head. "I'm sorry, but is that cat speaking?" She addressed the question to Dustin, who settled back into his chair and crossed an ankle up over his opposite knee.

"It's kind of rude to talk about someone as if they aren't there," Echo said. His voice was much deeper than she'd expect from such a tiny cat, and his mouth actually moved when he spoke. What was she thinking? She would never expect a cat to talk or have any preconceived notion of how deep of a voice one should have. Cas felt a wave of dizziness come over her again. It seemed like that was one of her body's responses to being overwhelmed with absurdity.

But it wouldn't do for anyone, even a cat, to think she was rude. "I'm sorry," she said her breath hitching. "I've never heard a cat talk before. I'm Cascade Lorne." She left her chair, crouched down in front of the cat, and held her hand out to him.

His eyelids narrowed to slits and he yawned again, but he made no move to give her his paw. After a few awkward seconds, she retracted her hand and stood up.

"This is Echo. He does errands for us sometimes. Well, when he feels like it, mainly." Dustin sounded cheerful now that his problem was solved. "Tallulah North lives at 1475 South Coast Road over in the Highlands subdivision. Echo will accompany you there. If you try to go anywhere else, we'll send a peacekeeper squad to nab you before you can move twenty steps.

Though his words were ominous, he said them in a friendly, matter-of-fact way. "We'll contact you once the council has figured out exactly what to do with you. In the meantime, I recommend you learn everything possible from your sister about controlling your magic."

Dustin jumped up from his chair with the ease of a man half his age, and Cas thought it was impressive for a man who must be at least sixty. He crossed to her, and she did her best to look him in the eye.

"Listen, you've been pretty nice to me, and I appreciate that. But I just have to say a couple of things. First, Tallulah is my *half*-sister," she emphasized the proper relationship with her tone. "Like I said, we aren't close, and I don't think she'll really welcome me with open arms. Second, I'm new to all of this, and I don't want to make a faux pas, but am I really expected to consider this cat my guardian? And, as far as that goes, *is* he my guardian or my prison guard?"

Dustin smiled and patted her shoulder. "I'm sorry, Ms. Lorne. I can only imagine how tough this day has been for you. Many humans would have passed out from the stress."

"Well, I did. Sort of," Cas mumbled. "But that's not going to happen again."

"Of course it isn't. You seem like a fine, strong person to me, and I think you'll get through this. But for right now, I would advise you to just keep your head down, do what the council says, and work on getting your power under control as quickly as possible. Those are the things that will keep you alive and un-banished for the next few days."

A buzz sounded in the room. "Yes?" Dustin said to the air.

Lavania's voice echoed into the room. "Please come to the council chambers. We need you to look up some precedents for us. Mr. Livings believes he should be able to put his luxury hotel right on the banks of the hot springs."

In the background, Cas could hear an angry voice. "I should be able to put my hotel up wherever I want to, right away! I make money for this town and for this council, and I can't believe how I'm being treated. I demand to be given my approval right now, so I can get started on this before my investors all get spooked."

"I'll be right there, Archsiren," Dustin said. The speaker buzzed off, drowning out the angry man in mid-sentence. "I have to go. Good luck, Ms. Lorne. And Echo," Dustin looked down at the cat and pointed an index finger at him. "You behave yourself or the council won't look kindly on it. Don't forget, we're keeping a close eye on you." With that, the clerk spun on his heel and left the room.

"Well, we'd better get going then. We can take a courser to within a block of South Coast Road—I think there's a stop in the bank over there. I'd better just use the little kitty's room before we go." Echo trotted over to a litter box with a hood, hopped in, and hunkered down. He looked over his shoulder and said, "Do you mind?"

"Oh, of course. Sorry." Cas felt awkward and turned away, busying herself looking at nature photographs on the wall. After a moment, she felt something brush against her leg.

Echo sauntered past. "I'm ready," he said. "Let's go."

Cas followed the cat out the door. She had mixed feelings as she stepped into the hallway. She was glad to be putting some distance between herself and the council, but she was nervous about going into public because of the unpredictable things that had been happening. And she was really not looking forward to seeing Tallulah.

Echo led her back out to the reception area where Waverly sat up on her high stool flipping through a magazine. She didn't look up at them when she spoke. "Stay in line, Echo."

"Stay awake, Waverly," Echo shot back, sarcasm dripping from his deep voice. "I know you're perpetually bored, but the council won't appreciate you falling asleep on the job."

The secretary rolled her eyes and flipped a magazine page.

Echo and Cas stepped out onto the round marble platform and rode it down to the building's lobby. It was busier than it had been when she and Juniper arrived. There were a lot of people in the lobby. Some of them stood in small groups chatting, others sat on benches that came out of the walls, reading papers and looking at phones, and some walked across the marble floor and stood on hover platforms that took them up to various levels of the Courthouse.

Cas followed Echo toward the front of the lobby, where a set of large glass doors framed the entrance. Sunlight poured in, highlighting twirling dust motes. Without warning, Cas sneezed.

Four small mice appeared in midair, confused looks on their tiny whiskered faces. They dropped to the ground and scattered. Echo bounded after the plumpest of the group. The mouse careened toward a crack in the foundation, wriggled into it, and was out of sight.

Echo sat down next to the hole and lifted his paw up to give it a few licks. Cas went over to him, and he bowed his head a little. "My apologies for that undignified behavior," he said, and his voice sounded remorseful. "Sometimes I can't control my urges."

"No problem. I'm not too good in that department either, right now. Sorry about creating or conjuring or producing those mice—I'm not sure what the right word is."

"Conjure is correct, I believe. I've been after that fat one for weeks. You probably kinetically brought them from their burrow to this space," Echo said. "Interesting. Were you hungry?"

"For mice? No, of course not."

"What were you thinking about, then?"

Cas shrugged. "A few seconds before, I was wondering if cats really eat mice or if that was a myth."

"I see," Echo said. "And then you bring mice to you." His green eyes roved over her from head to toe. "Interesting, new witch. Interesting. Ah, well. Come along. Let's get this mission done. Would you mind picking me up? I can't fit into the courser's seat belt, so lying on your lap will probably be safest for me."

"Sure." Cas picked the black cat up and before she could think about what she was doing, scratched him under his chin. "Oh, I'm so sorry, sir!" she exclaimed. "Is that rude?"

"A little unseemly, I suppose, but it feels quite nice. Please do continue." Echo began to purr a little as he settled into Cas' arms. "Now just walk over that way another few feet, and I'll call the courser."

Cas followed the cat's instructions and braced herself, waiting for the bubble to envelope her. As soon as it did, she leapt toward a chair and buckled herself in. She intended to avoid the dizziness this time. She grabbed a nose pincher and managed to get it on before the courser started moving.

Her quick preparations were quite effective, and this trip was much easier for her than the first one. The bubble stopped moving after only a moment or two—Cas realized that must be because they were just going across town this time.

When the courser disappeared, their feet hit beige carpet. They stood in a small business office, but before Cas could say anything, Echo jumped down from her arms and shooed her out of a door.

They were in a bank. Four tellers waited on customers. Cas glanced behind her. The door they'd exited was marked Burt Lierson, Manager. A cat walking across the bank's smooth, tiled floor didn't garner a second glance from anyone in the lobby. The security guard even tipped an imaginary hat at them as they exited.

"Who's Burt Lierson?"

"I don't know exactly. He may have existed at one point. Now witches use the office as a courser pick up and drop off. Can't have the humans noticing anything." Echo sniffed the air. "Ugh, wealthy people. Smells like corruption and unhappy, spoiled housewives. Come this way. It's just a few blocks."

South Coast Road proved to be a pretty street with tall oak trees planted in the strips of grass between the sidewalks and the road. Cas could see a few leaves starting to change color, though it would be another month before fall was fully upon them.

She turned around in a circle, taking in the huge, perfectly manicured lawns and giant, mansion-like houses of the neighborhood. It reminded her of TV reality shows about famous people in Hollywood. "I didn't know there was such a ritzy neighborhood here."

"Yes, the well-to-do of Crystal Springs do like to show off their wealth," Echo said, his voice full of contempt.

"How did Tallulah get to be well-to-do?" Cas marveled at the house closest to them, which had three turrets jutting up into the sky. They reminded her of fairytale towers where a maiden might be kept awaiting a prince.

"She's a motivational speaker. Mostly for humans. I don't understand why the review council hasn't dealt with her yet. She must be charming the humans because I've heard a couple of her speeches, and they're not that great. They didn't motivate me to do anything except drown my sorrows in a shot of bourbon."

Cas hadn't seen Tallulah in a long time, and she didn't know much about witch business, but she wouldn't put it past her half-sister to be gaming the system to her advantage. "Okay, well, let's get this over with. This one's 1473, so the next house on this side must be hers."

A WITCH TOO LATE 63

They arrived at a long driveway that led to an especially huge mansion. Cas didn't know much about architecture, but even her untrained eye could see that this house was a mismatched hodge-podge of styles. There was a pillared porch, multiple delicate spires, windows that looked quite modern, and the whole thing was pastel pink with white trim.

"Oh, this is horrible," she said under her breath.

"Someone has a lot of money and not a lot of style," Echo agreed, making Cas snort out a laugh.

They walked up to the door and rang the bell. They could hear the opening strains of Mozart's *The Magic Flute* play inside the house.

"Wow, pretentious much?" Echo muttered.

They had to ring the bell again before the tall door finally swept open, revealing a towering, red-haired man wearing a white tuxedo. "What can I do for you?" he asked, looking down his nose at Cas and Echo.

"We're here to see Tallulah North please," Cas said, smiling brightly.

"And who should I say is calling?" he asked, narrowing his eyes at her.

"Cascade Lorne." Her confidence slipped as she thought about how Tallulah probably wouldn't be that happy to see her, and she smiled harder to try and make up for it.

"Please come in, and I'll see if Miss North is available." He led them into a sitting room off the main foyer and left them there. The room was just as gaudy as the outside of the house, decorated with Picasso-like paintings in different shades of green paint, purple area rugs, and bright yellow furniture.

"If I had the right ears to hold them, I'd definitely put a pair of sunglasses on," Echo said, sounding disgusted.

"Yeah, it's over-the-top," Cas agreed.

"So they sent you anyway, I see."

The voice startled them. Cas spun around to face her half-sister. Tallulah had grown up to be about two heads taller than her, with a willowy figure and long, flowing blonde hair that Cas had always wished to have. Her makeup application was perfect, accentuating high cheekbones, long lashes, and full lips. Tallulah wore a floor-length, navy blue gown that sparkled when she moved. It was as if she was heading out to a red-carpet gala.

"I didn't answer their summons or phone calls for a reason, but the council never takes no for an answer." She swept past Cas, sitting down on the edge of a bright yellow couch, crossing her ankles, and laying her hands on her lap. "What do you need with me?"

Cas looked around for a place to sit. Nothing appeared comfortable, so she chose a yellow Queen Anne chair across from Tallulah. "Well, I've had quite a time of it over the past day. I'm having trouble making sense of it, but I was taken in front of a witch's council that seems to think I just blossomed. Strange things keep happening when I hiccup or sneeze, and they're saying I need a family member to stay with who knows about magic and can help me control my power. So they sent me to you. I didn't know you were even living here, Lu. How have you been?"

Tallulah's features didn't change or soften as she listened to Cas. She didn't react to the use of her childhood nickname either. "I'm great. As you can see, I have done quite well for myself." She lifted a hand and waved it around the room. "As for me helping you with your magic, I don't see how I can. I'm quite busy almost all the time with speaking engagements, small group classes, and individual mentoring. I'm hardly ever here, really."

Though she hadn't known she was holding out a small bit of skepticism on all this business about witches and magic, when her half-sister responded matter-of-factly about its existence, Cas felt a moment of shock followed by the click of acceptance. She had sneezed mice and flying pigs, was keeping company with a talking cat, and her long-lost half-sister seemed to accept magic as being real.

"How long have you had magic?" she asked.

Tallulah smoothed her hair and then examined her nails. "I blossomed when I was eleven. I guess you probably weren't aware of it. Dad didn't quite believe everything my Blossom Greeter explained, but he had no problem sending me away to Aunt Petunia after the council recommended it."

"Mom's sister? I remember you going there, and I didn't understand why he sent me to boarding school instead of to Aunt Petunia's with you. I was about thirteen, I guess. It was a hard pill for me to swallow—being sent away."

Tallulah's jaw muscles tightened as she clenched her teeth. "It wasn't any easier for me. Mom died before I could really remember her, then I had this magical thing happen that I didn't understand, and then I was sent away." She gave her head a tiny shake and stood up. "But, that's all in the past now, and there's nothing to be done for it. I wish I could help you, but I don't see how I can."

Cas didn't really want to stay in this gaudy house with her way-too-perfect half-sister. But her throat clenched at the idea of being sent away from the only family she had—the only one who might be able to understand what was happening and help her deal with it. She sniffed and lifted a hand toward Tallulah, intending to plead her case, but a small line of flame shot out of her fingertips. Cas squealed.

The fire landed on the yellow couch Tallulah had just vacated, and the upholstery smoldered. Tallulah screeched and started jumping around. She looped her forefingers together and snapped them apart. A grey rain cloud appeared over the couch. Rain dumped from it, dousing the fire. A burnt plastic smell hung in the air, and Tallulah's face looked hard and angry.

"I don't have time for this, Cascade. I am not a babysitter. I have a living to make. You need to go now."

"But..."

"No. I can't. The council is just going to have to clean up their own problems without my help." Tallulah turned on her heel. She swept out of the room in a cloud of blonde hair and navy-blue taffeta.

Chapter 6

Cas felt dazed as she and Echo made their way back to the courser at the bank. They rode it toward the Courthouse in silence. The entire experience with Tallulah had been unsettling. The idea that her half-sister had known the truth about their mother seemed unreal. But being rejected on top of that? It was almost too much to bear.

What was going to happen to her now?

Echo sat on Cas' lap and purred as she stroked him absent-mindedly. The courser's spin didn't even bother her. At least she'd adjusted to something well.

The purring stopped, and Echo glanced up. He could probably only really see Cas' nose pinchers from his angle, but it didn't stop him from interpreting the look on her face. "I'm sure it will be fine, Ms. Lorne. The council will come up with some way to help you."

"If they don't decide I'm too much trouble and call the executioners."

"Never mind that drivel from this morning," Echo said. "Most of the sirens were posturing. Your magical potential is quite substantial, and they're jealous. Killing a newspring at any age would be poor optics for the council. If anything, politics will keep you breathing for some time to come. None of them, including Lavania, want to lose their seat."

"If you say so, Echo. I wouldn't go back to the council at all if I could control..." Cas couldn't quite say it out loud. Her magic. It still seemed unreal and insane. She sounded miserable, and Echo was only trying to soothe her. Cas smiled at him. "Is the Archsiren always so irritable, or was it because she had to see me so early this morning?"

"Her husband ran off, so she's been in rare form ever since. Yet, Lavania is always unpleasant," the cat confirmed, his furry face twisting into what Cas assumed was a grimace. "It seems to be her nature, but I believe something in her past must have added to it. Most of the time, the other sirens keep her from being too over-the-top mean, but you do have to watch out for her."

Cas sighed. Lavania held her future in her hands, and she was crabby and short-tempered. Cas yawned, unable to stop herself. "Oh, I'm sorry," she said to Echo from behind her hand. "I'm starting to feel pretty exhausted."

"We'll take you back to the council, and hopefully, they'll be able to see you right away. Then I'm sure they'll let you rest."

The courser arrived at its destination, and Echo and Cas made their way over to the hover tile, up to the marble hallway, and into the reception area where Waverly looked like she hadn't budged since they left.

"We need to see the council again," Echo's deep voice rumbled at the receptionist.

Waverly set her magazine on her desk and stared down at the two of them. "Are you sure that's a good idea? You were supposed to leave her with her sister, but you've gone and brought her back. The Archsiren isn't going to be very happy about that."

"I'm aware of what my mission was, and it really isn't any of your business whether I completed it or not. Your job is to let the sirens know we need to see them and take us back to their chamber."

Silence filled the room as the blue-haired receptionist and the small black cat stared each other down. Cas shifted her feet and wondered if she should say something to break the tense atmosphere, but she couldn't think of anything. Finally, Waverly sighed, broke eye contact with Echo, and climbed down from her tall chair. "Fine. It's your funeral."

Cas and Echo followed Waverly back to the door leading to the council chambers. Cas' stomach did flips and her pulse started racing as they got closer. What would they do with her? Waverly stopped a few feet from the chamber door, and Cas followed so closely that she ran into the woman's back, earning herself a frosty, blue-eyed glare. "I'm sorry."

"Why did we stop?" Echo sauntered up from behind the two women and sat down next to Cas.

"Shh!" Waverly ordered and waved her hand at him.

As silence fell in the hallway, Cas could hear that there was an argument going on in the council chambers. She recognized the voice of the angry man she'd heard through the speaker back in Dustin's office that morning. What was his name? Lively? Livid? Livings! It was definitely him in there yelling, and he wasn't the only one. Lavania's voice was a shrill shriek between bursts of Livings' furious shouting. Cas strained to hear what was happening.

"Can I help you folks?"

The voice seemed to apparate next to her left ear. Cas jumped away from the sound and slammed into Waverly. The receptionist screeched and glared at Cas again.

A partially opaque wall appeared and floated about a foot above the floor and the same distance below the ceiling, situated between Cas' group and the speaker. It was silver and looked almost gauzy, but when Echo batted at it, his paw didn't go through or disturb it in any way. He cocked his head and looked up at Cas. "It's solid as steel but transparent enough to see through. Beautiful work."

Had she made the wall appear because she'd been startled? Was it like a shield or something?

On the other side of the strange floating wall was an even stranger looking person. It looked like a man with a long, drawn face and slicked back, shoulder-length hair. He wore a blue and green plaid bowtie and small round glasses. One eyebrow raised up above the rim of the glasses, changing his expression from serene to quizzical. The man's hands appeared very normal, though weathered. Within them, he held a small brown, leather-bound book. And for some reason, he didn't have any shoes on.

Actually, that wasn't quite accurate. Cas' mind shied away from it at first, but she had to acknowledge the truth. She'd never make it in this strange new world by using denial to cope.

It wasn't that he didn't have shoes. He didn't have feet. Or legs, really.

In fact, at the bottom of his neatly pressed gray suit coat, his body seemed to—end. He floated just like the wall she'd somehow conjured and was as eerily transparent.

"These two need to be brought before the council, Denzel. Where's Dustin?" Waverly asked the hovering half-man.

"He's attending to other matters. He didn't tell me exactly what those are, and I didn't ask. He's been doing quite a lot of work for the Founder's Day celebrations, so I assume it has to do with that. He asked me to fill in for him in his council duties for a few hours. Is this Cascade Lorne?"

Denzel cast his gaze at Cas, and she shivered when his eyes met hers. She hadn't been involved in the supernatural world for much more than twenty-four hours, but even she knew a ghost when she saw one. The wall she'd produced had disappeared and there was no longer anything standing between her and the hovering spirit. Cas wondered if she could make it return by wishing hard enough.

"Yes, that's her. I took her to her half-sister, but the miserable woman turned her away," Echo said nonchalantly. He looked up at Cas again. "My apologies. I didn't mean to be so blunt. But your sister's family values are worse than those of a tomcat in the middle of a pride of females. Turning her own sister away like that." He shook his furry head back and forth as though he'd never heard of such a thing before.

Waverly snorted. "Like your values are so pure," she muttered, and Echo hissed at her. The receptionist stuck her tongue out at the cat.

"Very well. I'll take them in, Waverly. You can go back to your desk. They'll have to wait here with me for a moment. The council is preoccupied with Dzovag Livings' case right now."

As though to punctuate the ghost assistant's words, Lavania's shrill voice rang out at that moment: "Dzovag, you are walking a thin line right now. I have half a mind to curse you out of existence! Get out of this chamber. We'll call you once we've decided your case. DENZEL!"

The ghost waved a hand and the chamber door opened. A middle-aged man with a thick paunch and overflowing jowls came stomping through it, almost running into Cas. "Get out of my way, girl," he growled.

Dzovag Livings looked so angry that if flames started shooting out of the top of his head, Cas wouldn't be surprised. He was dressed in an expensive blue suit tailored to fit his rotund body. The bright orange shirt and tie he wore with it made her eyes water.

He stopped and addressed Denzel, tiny bits of spit coming out of his mouth as he spoke. "It's pure incompetence in there, just as I expected. And now a threat from the Archsiren. I never! You heard her threaten me, didn't you? None of you in this office know what you're doing. You clearly need a new leader. Tell Dustin to call me when he gets back from wherever he's gotten off to. I want to lodge a formal complaint." Without waiting for the ghost to acknowledge his order, Dzovag stomped off down the hallway and into the reception area. Cas felt sorry for Waverly for a second, since she'd have to deal with him out there.

"Lavania!" The words yanked Cas' attention back to the open door of the Council chamber. She could see Lavania and part of Albert from where she stood but not the other three sirens. "Control yourself. Livings might be unpleasant, but he's not worth having to go in front of the Tribunal for because you've killed him without due process. We all need to decide together what we should do about his request. Personally, I don't think his new hotel would be such a bad thing."

"Not a bad thing? Right on the banks of the hot springs where the humans it would attract might interfere with our fire element? Shiloh, you are the most incompetent nincompoop of a siren we've ever had on this council! I've been hoping for ages that you'd step down on your own, but you aren't bright enough to do so." Lavania appeared livid, and her severe features were drawn back so far she started to resemble a skeleton.

"Honestly, Lavania. Now you've gone and made her cry," Albert croaked. Cas could see him reach a papery hand in Shiloh's direction. "Shush, shush. She's just angry. Don't take her seriously."

"I am serious, Albert, and you should be too. This hotel is a terrible thing for Crystal Springs, and I need to rely on all of you to help me stop it."

"We haven't had enough time to discuss it yet." Valencia's voice sounded calm and rational. "Let's take a break and reconvene in a few hours. Maybe then, clearer heads will prevail."

"None of you have clear heads. I'm the only one on this council using their brain today. I don't care what any of you has to say about it. That hotel is not going up, no matter what I have to do to stop it."

Lavania stepped down from her chair, which disappeared back into the wall, and marched out of the room. She passed Cas without a glance. Albert and Valencia followed her out, flanking a sobbing Shiloh. They paused to put their heads close to Denzel, though Cas couldn't hear what they said. The three sirens continued on, disappearing through a doorway between the council chamber and the reception room door.

"Come along," Denzel said, and Cas and Echo followed him into the chamber. Stu sat on his chair staring at his knees. Denzel cleared his throat, and the siren raised his head. "Sir, Echo has returned with Ms. Lorne, and they require further direction from the council."

Stu barked out a short laugh. "The council is a little scattered right now."

"Sirens Albert and Valencia instructed me to have you make a decision in their stead, sir. They said to assume they vote with you, so you have a 3/5 majority to do as you wish with the newspring."

Stu laughed again. "Well, why not?" His eyes moved to Cas. "I suppose someone has to deal with you. What happened with your sister?"

"My *half*-sister and I had a short talk, and then she told me she couldn't help me." Cas decided not to report the part where Tallulah said the council would have to deal with its own problems. It seemed inflammatory, and the last thing she wanted was to make this handsome siren upset when he held her fate entirely in his hands.

"Hmm. Not very helpful, is she? Well, I guess we shouldn't have expected much more. She has a history of doing things her own way." Stu tipped his head to the side as he looked at Cas. He chewed on his bottom lip for a second. "How long was it since you saw her again? Before today?"

"Her dad—my step-dad—sent her away to live with our Aunt Petunia when she blossomed. I was thirteen, so that would have been . . ."

"Your aunt?" Stu's head straightened, and his eyebrows went up. "Is she magical?"

"Yes, I guess so. That's what I understand, anyway," Cas affirmed.

"Is she local?"

Cas glanced at the ghost. Dustin hadn't mentioned any other living relatives during the earlier council session. "I don't know. Maybe?

"Well, there we go. We'll send you to her for safe-keeping. I don't think we've gotten a report from the peacekeeper squad we sent to your house to find the stone yet. Denzel, please find out where the aunt lives so Echo can take her there. When is Dustin going to be back?"

"In a few hours, I believe, sir."

"Yes, okay. I'm sure he's doing something for Founder's Day. Boy, we could all use a good celebration. I'm getting together with some witches who are coming into town for the festivities. If we can keep the sirens from cursing each other until the drinks start flowing tonight, we should be good, eh?"

Stu climbed down from his chair while speaking and clapped a hand on Denzel's shoulder, but his fingers passed through the assistant's wispy body. The ghost merely nodded.

Stu left the room before Cas could say anything else. She was relieved that she hadn't been cursed or sent to Sitegard or anything, but the thought of visiting her aunt made her feel uneasy. "I haven't seen Aunt Petunia in decades," she said. "I guess I blamed her along with my step-dad when Tallulah was sent to her and I had to go to boarding school. I wonder what she's like now."

"I guess we'll find out," Echo said matter-of-factly. He sounded eager to get going.

"She lives at 14 Crowhead Lane," Denzel said from across the room, reading a large, open book. "Same house she lived in when Ms. Lorne's half-sister stayed with her."

Cas felt a rush of gratitude toward the assistant for remembering to add the *half*. It was a petty thing to insist on, but Tallulah had never been a pleasant person. Saying they were connected by one parent made Cas feel better—as if it somehow added a layer of separation between them.

Gratitude toward a ghost? Cas hoped she wasn't losing her mind. On the heels of that emotion, another wave of exhaustion overcame her.

"Crowhead. Crowhead. I don't think I know where that is. Which courser do we take?" Echo asked.

"The one to the old lodge," Denzel replied. "It's abandoned and up for sale, so the humans aren't using it right now. Take the courser there and walk four blocks up Serene Street to Crowhead. It will be the fourth house on your right, I believe."

"Thanks, good sir. We'll see you later." Echo headed toward the hallway, and Cas followed him.

They were silent as they made their way back through reception, past Waverly, down the hover-lift, and across to the courser stop on the main floor. Cas picked Echo up without remark, and he called the courser. When it stopped after their ride and let them off, they were inside an empty ski lodge lobby.

The lodge was built with logs, and hardwood floors ran throughout the entire lobby. One wall was covered with a giant fireplace surrounded by beautiful stonework. A long desk, also made of logs, sat to one side, and skis and boots hung on the wall opposite the fireplace. Cas couldn't imagine the skill it had taken for someone to carve the logs that made up the rails of the spiral staircase in the center of the room.

There were several cozy sitting areas, and the wall behind the desk was entirely glass. It looked out on a slope that was covered with greenery now, but Cas knew that winter's snow would transform it into a formidable ski hill.

"Wow, this place is nice," Cas breathed.

"I suppose," Echo sounded bored. "It reeks of mildew."

"True." The air was warm and dank inside the lodge. None of the furniture had been covered. Who knew what was growing in here. It looked as if one day someone had locked the doors and walked away. Everything was covered in a thin layer of dust. "It could use a good cleaning and airing out, I guess. Get some new furniture and can you imagine it all decorated for Christmas, with a giant tree right over there?" Cas gestured to one side of the room.

"It's for sale, you know." Echo jumped out of Cas' arms and headed for the door.

Cas followed him, still rubber-necking to take in all the details of the beautiful lobby. "I'm sure it's a million dollars. But oh, wouldn't it be fun to own a place like this?"

They stepped outside, and Echo looked around for a moment to get his bearings before trotting off down the sidewalk. "It might not be too much money. It's small, and the owners might want to unload it. If you're interested, you should check it out when this is all over."

When this is all over? What did that mean? From what Cas could tell, her life would never be the same. Not so long ago, she had wanted some adventure. Now, she just wanted a quiet night sipping wine on her back porch.

"No, I don't think so, Echo. This place is for someone who gets this world, and I don't think that's me," Cas said.

It didn't take long for them to arrive at 14 Crowhead Lane. The house was a tiny, mint green bungalow with white shutters and a tidy walkway. Cas hesitated for a second and took a deep breath. "Well, no use dragging this out, I guess." She walked up to the door and knocked.

She had to knock two more times before the door opened a crack. An eye peered out from under the safety chain. Above the orb was a short forehead and a shock of white hair. Below it was a delicate nose and bright red lipstick that hadn't quite managed to land entirely on the lady's lips. "Who are you?" she croaked.

"Aunt Petunia, it's Cascade." Cas smiled as warmly as possible. She hoped her mother's sister would recognize her.

Instead, nothing happened. The eye continued to stare, but the door didn't open further. The woman's face didn't twitch. Maybe she was hard of hearing.

"CASCADE," she said louder and smiled again.

The door slammed shut, and she jumped. Cas glanced down at Echo. She couldn't believe she'd been rejected by another family member. Two in one day was a little much for anyone to handle.

Then Cas heard the clanking of a chain and the door opened. She could see her aunt's whole face now, plastered with a grin that was almost as wide as her open arms. "My dear!" the old lady cried. "I've missed you so! Come in, come in. Give your auntie a hug."

Cas stepped forward into her aunt's embrace and closed her eyes. Perhaps things were going to work out after all.

Chapter 7

Cas stepped out of the embrace and smiled into her aunt's kind face. The lady smiled back, though her haphazard lipstick made it look clownish. They stood there smiling at each other for a few moments before Petunia spoke. "You're very pretty, dear. Who are you?"

Cas blinked and felt her smile slip away. "Um. I'm Cascade Lorne. Your sister's daughter."

"Oh, that's right!" Petunia's face lit up for a moment but then it fell again as she shook her head and made tsk-tsk noises. "It's a wonder you turned out so good, considering what your mother did. Getting into trouble with those friends of hers all the time—yes, a bad deal for you for sure."

She frowned, sighed, and shook her head again.

Cas cast a sidelong look down at Echo. What was that bit about her mother? But before she could gather her swirling thoughts and ask for more details, Petunia said, "Ah, well, that's all over now, rest her soul. Come in, dear. I'll make us some nice tea and cookies."

Petunia turned and walked into the front hallway of the bungalow, which looked dark and a little uninviting to Cas from the front stoop. She glanced down to make sure Echo was with her before she moved forward.

The sight of the short hallway they entered was alarming. It had a slight odor, like cheese left in the fridge for too long.

Cas stepped over a green polka-dot umbrella missing half its canopy. Shoes of different sizes littered the space. Men's shoes, ladies high heel pumps, and flip-flops in various colors lay where they'd been tossed. But from what Cas could see, not one of them had a match. Then there were the hats. For some reason, they were in pairs, tacked along the wall in a haphazard pattern.

Echo sniffed at a man's sneaker as large as his head. "Huh, what do you know? Entraps."

"No, what do I know?" Cas answered in a hush tone. Her heart had picked up an extra beat. This hallway didn't bode well.

"It's nothing, really. Your auntie has a flair for storing spells in everyday objects. Apparently, she has a thing for shoes." Echo craned his neck to look up. "And headwear. Let's hope she didn't study with the necromancy guild. Who knows what we'll find in the kitchen."

Cas' shoulder brushed against a black-checkered sunhat and sent up a cloud of dust. She sneezed.

Petunia called over her shoulder, "Be mindful of the hats, dear. They get frisky."

Cas didn't know how a hat could get frisky. But she cast a wary eye back at the sunhat. The thing shivered as the wide brim curved to form a smile.

"Here we are, dears," Aunt Petunia said as she entered the kitchen. "Much nicer in here. I keep old, pesky incantations in the hallway. They tend to build up like junk mail." Petunia moved over to a yellow gas stove.

"This is better," Cas said under her breath as they stepped into the new room. She breathed a sigh of relief at the sight of a small, yet uncluttered kitchen filled with natural light. The double set of windows were even framed with frilly curtains decorated with marigolds.

Movement caught Cas' eye. She watched in amazement as a straw broom with a wooden handle danced its way across the floor. It skirted around her and Echo before moving on to get some crumbs from under a tiny kitchen table.

The broom wasn't the only thing in the kitchen moving on its own. A giant knife sliced fresh bread, and sandwich fixings floated out of the refrigerator to land on the countertop next to it. A dish sponge soaped plates in the sink.

Despite very ordinary things performing actions that weren't ordinary at all, Cas felt the kitchen was very pleasant and homey.

Petunia sat down on a bar stool to watch the knife work, and she glanced back at her visitors. "Would you like a roast beef sandwich?" she asked them in a kind tone.

"Yes," Echo answered without hesitation, jumping onto the stool next to the old lady.

"Sure," Cas said, a little hesitant. "I don't remember when I ate last."

Petunia peered at her and tsk-tsked again. "You do look a little frail, dear. We can't have that. Your dear mother would want me to feed her daughter well. Sit down here, and I'll get you a nice, thick sandwich."

"Okay. Thank you. Um, could you explain what you said before about my mother? Something about it being a shame I have to deal with what she did?" Cas felt a surge of anxiety, fearing Petunia would reveal something horrible about her mother. Suddenly, the knife stopped slicing bread. It hovered in midair, shivering a little.

"What on Earth?" Petunia said. Her forehead scrunched. The wild lipstick around the top of her mouth looked like it was heading up into her nose as her lips pursed. She slapped the counter. "Stop that, knife. What's wrong with you today?"

As if answering, the knife hovered for another millisecond before it shot across the room, whizzed past Cas' ear, and dove toward the broom handle. The broom seemed to sense the incoming danger. It dodged and careened across the room, the knife following closely. The broom knocked things off shelves and left a cloud of dust as it desperately tried to evade certain impalement.

Petunia screeched, placed one hand atop the other, and flicked her wrists in unison. But nothing happened. "I know these spells better than a dog knows bones. What. Is. Going. On?"

She repeated the motion once, twice, three times. Each time became more urgent than the last. But Petunia couldn't reclaim control of the household spells she'd placed on the knife and the broom.

In fact, things only seemed to get worse. The soapy water in the sink began to swirl like a whirlpool. Dishes shot across the room like out-of-control missiles. They crashed and broke on the floor.

Cas shrieked and ran for cover under the tiny table. Not that it provided much protection.

As if in response, the dishes flung themselves out of the sink, and the knife chased the broom at a more fevered pitch.

"I think this might be you, Ms. Lorne," Echo said as he climbed onto the counter. He dodged a flying coffee cup before snagging a slice of roast beef and hauling it back to safety under the table. He dropped it. "You must calm yourself."

Cas pushed herself further under the table. "What? Me? I'm not doing this!"

"No, but I suspect you're disrupting your auntie's spells. I can smell your anxiety and spurts of magic coming off you." He chomped down on the roast beef as the broom handle narrowly missed clocking him in the ear.

"Ach! My home! My kitchen! My things! They're all getting ruined!" Petunia screamed as she hopped around the kitchen. Her hands swung in the air. "You must be a demon!" she shot at Cas. "Who are you, anyway? Why are you here? Get out, get out!"

"Aunt Petunia, it's me, Cascade. I'm so sorry about this."

"Cascade? Why, she's only a little girl! You can't be her. Tallulah!" She shouted the name louder than Cas would have thought possible for someone of her height. "Come down here and help me get these demons out of the house! They've ruined my spells!"

Cas and Echo exchanged glances. "We'd better go," Echo said, and Cas nodded.

The dishes had finally stopped flying out of the sink. Cas made a break for it when the knife chased the broom to the far edge of the kitchen.

Cas' stomach clenched as she realized this was the last family member she knew of. No one was coming to her rescue. As the broom escaped and renewed its scramble to avoid being impaled, Cas said, "Aunt Petunia, I'm so sorry about this. I'll leave so you can put it all right again. Take care."

Petunia didn't answer. She was too busy making wild leaps to catch the knife by its handle as it flew past her.

They exited the house, leaving the chaos of the out-of-control spells behind. "Now what?" Defeated, Cas flopped down on the front step of the house.

"Back to the council, I suppose. I'm sorry, Ms. Lorne." Echo licked his chops, dragging a tiny errant piece of roast beef into his mouth with his rough tongue.

Cas covered her face with one hand and leaned on an elbow. "I'm sorry. I don't mean to whine. I'm just so tired and confused and aggravated. But you're right, I know. Back we go." She looked up to focus on Echo.

Echo flicked out a paw and commenced with a quick bath. Cas swallowed her irritation. She was asking a cat what she should do. This was madness. Instead of saying something snippy, she looked around the area for the first time. On the way there, her mind had been preoccupied.

The bungalow was on the edge of a copse. Further up the street, Cas could see neighboring houses that were all small one levels like her aunt's. This place looked normal, just like her own neighborhood.

A loud crash issued from inside Petunia's house. Cas groaned out loud. Were the neighbors witches too? Were odd goings-on the norm and would they ignore it?

Cas had no interest in sticking around to find out. The last thing she wanted was a mob of angry, magic-wielding witches.

She rose to her feet. "How far of a walk is it? The fresh air might do my nerves some good."

"It's across town, so it would probably take us well over an hour to walk. But we could take the courser half way and then walk the rest of the way to the Courthouse," Echo replied. "You calming your nerves would be beneficial to us both."

Cas wasn't sure, but she thought the cat smirked with his last sentence.

She chose to ignore it. Right now, she felt like a menace. Even Cas couldn't fault a talking cat who didn't want to be around her. "That sounds good. I'm sure the council will be thrilled to see me. Again. Let's go tempt fate and hear what they'll say now. Maybe they'll choose not to kill me. Again."

Tingles shot across her hands. She turned one palm up. Tiny orange bolts of crackling energy jumped between her fingers. Cas shut her eyes and opened them. The little lightning bolts were gone. Part of her wanted to pretend it had been a figment of her imagination. But no, after all that had happened, Cas couldn't pretend anymore.

Emotions triggered her magic. Huh. Well, that knowledge was better than nothing. The key, then, was to keep herself in check. The thought made her feel just a tad more in control as she followed Echo down the sidewalk.

The courser pickup point on this side of town was in a dilapidated shack that appeared to have been a garage in a former life. Weather-beaten shingles dangled off the roof. Bits of old white-wash flecked the wooden exterior but most of it had faded to a general shade of grey-rot.

Echo nudged the door open with a paw. Cas prepped herself for a dank room with ancient spider webs hanging in the corners.

The cat sauntered in a few feet and sat on his haunches. "Surprised?"

She nodded. "Yeah, definitely."

"Courser ports have to be inconspicuous to discourage humans from coming too close," he said. "We set wards to keep them at bay, of course, but every bit helps."

Where the exterior indicated this was a forgotten relic, the inside was as if time hadn't passed. It was a simple garage painted a pristine white. Even the floor shone from an unseen light source. An immaculate 1950's Chevy occupied one of two spaces intended for a car.

"This place is bigger than the outside," Cas said and turned to peek outside the door.

"Magic, Ms. Lorne. You'll have to get used to it." Echo tapped at his collar to call their ride.

Cas pointed. "So is that car really there or is that some magical hologram or something?"

Even with a short snout, Echo managed a snort. "Of course it's real. But just for show. I doubt it's functional. A few years back, there was a whole thing to make the more active courser ports attractive in addition to functional. The younger, richer witches like Stu want everything to be pretty. Ah, here's our ride."

The trip was quick. Quicker than Cas liked. When the courser stopped its spin, dozens of glassy eyes peered through the translucent skin of the bubble. It was more than eyes—there was also fur, antlers, and long, thick black claws.

"I know, I know. Just move outside the shop quickly." Echo leaped from the courser.

They emerged out into the street. Cas turned to read the sign painted onto the door.

"Taxidermy?"

Echo arched his back in a nice stretch. "It's not my favorite incantation. Courser ports this close to town are disguised as businesses that go out of business every few months. This time round, someone chose a taxidermist as the guise. As you can imagine, it's not the top choice for a cat."

"But that's not a good choice. There's plenty of hunting and fishing nearby. The humans who hunt would come here."

"Between you and me, it hasn't been a popular choice amongst the community. The humans have tripped off the wards and they've had to be redone several times already. Rumor is Shiloh chose the guise and Lavania has been chiding her almost constantly about it. Rupol's Taxidermy may be going out of business sooner than expected as result," Echo said. "This way to the Courthouse."

They were on one of Crystal Springs' main streets—Morgana Avenue. It was a shop-lined area featuring everything from homemade ice cream to a mom and pop hardware store. Cas had been in the town's proper many times, but she'd never suspected anything strange here.

Cas walked a step or two behind Echo. He flicked the tip of his tail from side to side as he padded along the sidewalk. Echo didn't garner as many second glances as Cas would've guessed. But he also wasn't talking at the moment.

How many of these people were witches? A woman and a boy around six exited a barber shop. Were they magical?

What about that guy putting money into the parking meter? Or the woman walking her dog? Or the old man buying fruit at the shop on the corner?

Cas had no way of knowing. She peered, though discreetly, into every face that passed by. Everyone seemed normal. No not normal. Ordinary. But didn't she herself seem ordinary? And if not, what did that make her now?

Car traffic along Morgana was steady. Cas stared at the drivers and passengers alike. The faces ranged from bored to happy, from brown-skinned to pale. Flashes of witches flying on brooms popped into her mind's eye. Did they even drive cars?

What did having magic mean? If experience had taught her anything, nothing came for free. There was a price to pay for all things.

What would be her price?

The thought twisted her belly into one large, hard knot. After the separation from her husband, life had been turned upside down. No, that wasn't completely true. Life had been a screaming rolling-coaster of moving from one dramatic incident to another, all caused by her gambling addicted ex. But when the ink dried on the divorce papers, she'd faced the gaping maw of a dark unknown. Who was she?

The last few months had been a sometimes-agonizing puzzle of putting herself back together. And only recently had Cas begun to feel a semblance of normal. She hadn't known it just a few hours ago, but pondering paint colors had been a blessing in disguise.

And she'd had the audacity to dream of something more. Of adventure.

Well, adventure had literally walked up to the front door and handed her a package. What had she been doing ever since that moment?

Freaking out. That's what.

"What am I going to do?" she said under her breath.

Echo stopped in his tracks. He glanced around before speaking. "Ms. Lorne, I'm feeling a surge. I urge you to think serene thoughts."

They paused at an intersection to wait for the pedestrian light to turn green.

A car's horn beeped. Cascade jumped and let out a shriek.

The hair on Echo's back stood up straight. "Ms. Lorne! Please! We can't afford an incident here."

Cascade wrapped her arms around herself. "Sorry, sorry. I'm on edge. Aunt Petunia didn't do much for my nerves." As she thought about her aunt, an odd feeling started to rise from her toes. It was as if the ground under her feet trembled and began to travel up her legs. "Do you feel that, Echo?"

The cat stood up on his hind legs and leaned his front paws against Cas' shins. "Ms. Lorne! Calm down. I can feel—"

The tremble rolled upward faster and faster. Then it was inside her head, filling it with what felt like champagne bubbles.

All at once, the bubbles began to pop.

Fireworks erupted in the center of the intersection. Car tires screeched as a blue mini-van swerved to miss the noise and lights. More screeching tires followed as the orderly traffic procession through the intersection devolved into a chaotic mess of lurching cars and near misses.

Cas clapped a hand over her mouth. If she caused an accident, she'd never forgive herself.

After a moment, all the cars in the area stopped. The smell of burning rubber hung in the air. People shouted at each other and shook their fists. They didn't know what had triggered the near accident but settled for blaming each other.

What had she done? Horrified, Cas wondered if she could somehow diffuse the situation. She stepped off the curb only to find the path blocked.

Echo swatted at her ankle. "I know what you are thinking. And the answer is no. You cannot help. We need to go straight to the sirens."

Cas opened her mouth to argue. At the same moment, a movement across the intersection caught her eye. A woman with long, auburn hair walked quickly, ignoring the cars and shouting people in the middle of the street.

It was the woman she'd seen several times in her neighborhood—the one she'd asked Mr. Percy about. What were the chances she'd be in Crystal Springs at this instant?

A strained voice coming from the general area of her ankles brought her back to the present.

"We should depart, Ms. Lorne," Echo pronounced in a stern tone. She looked down at him, and when she looked back, the mysterious woman was out of sight.

"My job is to keep track of you and make sure you don't cause any havoc, and here I've gone and let you almost cause a twelve car pileup. Let's not mention this little incident to the sirens, all right?"

"Yes, that's a good idea," Cas replied. There was no hurry to give the council more reasons to kill or banish her.

"Just don't do anything, okay? Don't think. Don't even breathe unless it's necessary. Let's get to the Courthouse as quickly as possible." Echo deftly began to maneuver around angry drivers and stalled cars.

It was harder for Cas to get through because she was about a thousand times Echo's size, but she made it and managed not to sniff, sneeze, hiccup, or cough again.

Cas felt some déjà vu as they re-entered the Courthouse lobby. How many times would she have to come back here before something could really be done? She hoped the peacekeepers had found the stone since she'd been here last. Maybe with that, the sirens could figure out what was going on and help her. She longed to go home.

Waverly wasn't there when they got to the reception area. Instead, Denzel floated behind her desk. He looked up at them when they entered and smiled. *Yikes.* Cas decided she much preferred Waverly's air of detached boredom, over this ghostly, grinning attempt at friendliness. It came off as macabre.

"What happened at the aunt's house?" he inquired.

"Let's just say the aunt is a no-go. We'll need to go before the council again," Echo answered.

Denzel paused long enough to size the woman and cat up. He peered over the rim of his glasses. "Very well. I'll let them know."

Denzel floated through the wall behind the desk and disappeared for a few minutes. He re-entered the room the traditional way when Dustin opened the door and came through with him.

"Well, well. Looks who's back. I heard you were here earlier too. Seems like you can't stay away." Dustin's words were cutting, but his smile and light tone took the edge off.

"My aunt couldn't remember who I was for more than a few minutes," Cas said. She decided to leave out the entire spells-gone-crazy mishap.

"That's a tough break. Well, we'll have to see if the sirens can figure something else out for you. They're on lunch break right now, but they're in chambers, so I'm sure they'll see you. Come on, I'll take you. Denzel, can you please keep holding down the fort out here until Waverly comes back from lunch?"

"Of course, sir," the ghost replied. He hovered behind the desk again.

Dustin led Cas and Echo down the marble hallway to the council chambers and opened the door. All five sirens were in their chairs.

Shiloh looked sullen and kept casting sidelong glares at Lavania. Some of the sirens munched on food. Stu read a paperback book with a western scene on the cover. They all looked up when the three newcomers arrived.

"What are they doing back here again?" Lavania sounded exasperated.

"It seems as though Ms. Lorne's aunt is no longer of very sound mind," Dustin explained.

"How so?" the Archsiren asked sharply. "Echo, what happened?"

"The old woman knew who Ms. Lorne was when we told her, but she kept having to be reminded. Toward the end of our visit, she seemed to revert to an earlier time in her life.

She thought that Ms. Lorne and her half-sister were younglings again." Echo sat down and lifted a paw to lick at it.

Lavania leveled a stare, first at the cat, then at Cas. "And? I can tell from your demeanor that's not all. Did something else happen?"

Cas shifted her weight and exchanged glances with Echo. She didn't want him to feel the need to lie for her or face penalties for keeping information from the council. She bit her lower lip. It made her nervous to explain what happened. Maybe when they heard about the eruption of power she'd had, they'd get angry and punish her.

But at this point, she was beyond caring much. Forget it. Tell the truth.

"I got a little upset and must have let off some magic or something," she said, and her voice cracked a little. "It made Aunt Petunia's household spells go haywire, and that upset her."

"See? She can't be trusted! All that power and no way to control it. And the peacekeepers haven't found the stone she claims SunSprite brought her yet. What a disaster. This woman must be contained!" Albert squawked and shook his cane at Cas.

Cas backed up a step, overwhelmed by the sudden venom the old siren directed at her. But then she straightened her back and looked Albert in the eye.

"I'm getting tired of being threatened. Send me home, and we all can be done with each other. If I don't have family to take care of me. I'll take care of myself. Send me home with a manual or a grimoire or something, and I'll figure this out on my own."

Lavania put down a forkful of salad. "If you're no witch, how do you know of grimoires?"

Cas forced herself not to smirk. "Television, lady."

The Archsiren sat back in her chair and templed her fingers. "Finally, a spark of your mother's spirit. I was beginning to wonder."

"There's another way to contain her," Shiloh spoke up. Lavania rolled her eyes in the woman's direction, but the younger siren pulled something out of her pocket. "Though it is a tad... unorthodox."

Stu slapped his paperback shut. "Tell me you didn't."

"Even with mentors, Cascade was going to require serious intervention for the near future. The council must not look bad in the eyes of the community. So, yes. I did."

Valencia leaned over, trying to look at the thing in Shiloh's palm. "What did you do?"

"She contacted Mortimer, that's what she did," Stu answered and crossed his arms. "We discussed this—"

"—and I decided to take action." Shiloh cut him off. "Now, before you all get excited, I made a very discreet call..."

The order of the council devolved as they all began to speak over one another. Cas' brow furrowed as she struggled to follow the conversation.

Cas leaned over and whispered to the cat sitting by her feet. "Um, Echo? What's going on?"

"It seems," Echo said, unable to hide the surprise in his voice, "the siren Shiloh called on a black market dealer."

"Oh." Cas straightened just as Lavania clapped her hands for them to come back to order.

A WITCH TOO LATE

The Archsiren's mouth looked like a thin, hard line. She shot Shiloh a final withering glance before speaking to the council. "Though brash, I agree with Shiloh's assessment."

"But Lavania—" Valencia started.

"Silence. I'm weary of all this discussion." She rubbed her forehead as if a headache was coming on. "And I'm particularly tired of you, Ms. Lorne." She paused and appeared deep in thought for a moment. "Very well, let's take a vote. Is anyone opposed to using this item?"

Lavania stared down each siren, but no one voiced an objection. "Very well. Dustin, place it on her.

Cas could feel the muscles in her neck tighten. "Put what on me?" Whatever it was remained hidden in Shiloh's grasp.

Dustin retrieved the object. His back was turned, and Cas could see how he looked down and inspected it. He cleared his throat. "Forgive my impudence again, but I think the siren's decision is a good one. With this, Ms. Lorne may go home with minimal supervision. I think she could use some rest."

"Enough with the brown-nosing, Dustin. Just put the thing on her," Lavania snapped.

Dustin bowed in acquiescence. He crossed back to Cas.

She started to feel a tremor beneath her feet. It was building ever so slowly.

Dustin must have seen something on her face. "It's okay, Ms. Lorne." He opened his hand. On top of his palm rested an oval, orange gemstone attached to a thick silver chain.

"This is a dousing amulet. It's very taboo in the witching community, which is why Siren Shiloh had to use very unorthodox means to obtain it. It won't hurt a bit. See, I'll demonstrate."

Dustin looped the chain over his head. Behind him, more than one of the sirens gasped. He flashed a satisfied grin over his shoulder before turning back to Cas. "See, it doesn't hurt at all."

"So then why are the sirens so freaked out?" Cas asked.

He jingled the chain. "There's quite a bit of superstition about items that tamper with a witch's magical strength. But for a witch of your magnitude, this will only subdue your power. It'll keep you and the people around you safe. No more flying pigs or paper hearts when you sneeze." Dustin slipped the amulet off and held it out. "May I?"

Cas' gaze swept the room and landed on Echo. The cat only peered back. This decision would have to be hers alone. Could she trust them?

Well, she *had* just caused a multi-car pileup in the middle of town.

"I don't have much of a choice." Cas stepped forward

Dustin flashed the warm smile again and put the chain over Cas' head.

The change was instant. The tremble that had been inching up her body snapped off like shutting a faucet, though she did feel strange too. It was as if everything in the room had become a bit muted or covered with a thin sheen of grey. It was odd but tolerable. For the first time all day, she relaxed. The thought that she could hiccup or cough without causing a fire or a flood was reassuring.

"What of the stone, Dustin?"

Dustin gave Cas a reassuring wink before turning back to the council. "Archsiren, the peacekeepers have yet to find anything, though there are residual signs that something odd did take place. They are investigating other aspects of Ms. Lorne's story."

Lavania drummed pointy nails against her armrest. "If the thing exists, we can't have it at large. If something of such magical value fell into nefarious hands, the results would be catastrophic for us."

Once again, Dustin bowed. "I will direct the search myself, Archsiren, and report to you immediately about any developments."

The offer didn't seem to relieve Lavania. Distracted, she dug a fingernail into the wood of the chair, gouging out a small groove. Without warning, she stood and left the audience chamber through a side door.

"I guess that's that," Albert said and stood to go as well.

Shiloh spoke up. "Echo, go with Ms. Lorne. Keep an eye on her. If the stone shows up, report back to us immediately."

"And if she manages to use any magic, you better be back here in an instant to let us know." Valencia wrinkled her nose as if she smelled something rotten. "All this drama is giving me indigestion. Go. All of you."

Cas thought a thank you was in order. But with Valencia's decree, the sirens who were left had already lost interest in them. Except Stu, who winked over the book he'd reopened.

Dustin ushered them out of the council chambers and back to the reception area. "Time for you to go home and get some rest. Just do your normal thing, and we'll contact you once we have any new information," he told her.

Cas nodded. "Thank you for all of your help."

"You're welcome. I like you. You're spunky." Dustin turned his attention to Echo. "I know you haven't been out of Crystal

Springs for a while. Don't get any bright ideas. Stay with Cas and keep an eye on things."

"Of course. I would never consider doing anything else," the cat said with a haughty flick of the tail.

As Cas and Echo settled into the chair in the courser to head back to her house, Cas closed her eyes and let her shoulders relax.

Home.

Outside, colors zipped by as the courser traveled at a speed she couldn't comprehend. In her lap, Echo nibbled at something caught between his toes.

Cas was going home all right. She was going home in a magic bubble with a talking cat.

Just a few hours earlier, Cas had thought going home would make everything better. Life would go back to normal. Now, a sinking feeling in her stomach said something different.

Cas pushed the dismal feeling aside. She was bone tired but knew sleep would be impossible until she'd had some time to process everything that had happened. That was just fine with her.

At least she'd be safe at home, and the craziness would be over.

Chapter 8

Despite Cas' feelings of trepidation about the future, it felt so good to be home. She always leaned a tiny bit toward being a homebody. She liked to read, cook, and watch light-hearted romantic comedies with some popcorn and a glass of wine. She always felt happy when she returned home from being out. But this homecoming was sweeter than any she remembered. It felt as though she'd been gone for a month instead of a day.

"I'll give you the grand tour, and then I'm going to take a long, hot shower," she told Echo. She showed him her small house. "You can stay in my guest room. You can sleep up on the bed; it's really cozy."

She found an old plastic sweater box, filled it with sand from her backyard, and tucked it into the closet for him. "I'm sorry it doesn't have a hood, but you'll have lots of privacy in there," she explained. "Tomorrow, I'll get a proper box for you."

Echo sniffed at the sand. "And please procure some scented litter. Scoopable. I'm not a heathen, you know. Do you have any paté?"

"I think I have some rotisserie chicken. I'll get some for you."

Once she had gotten Echo settled, satisfied and purring over the chicken, Cas hopped in the shower and stayed in there until the water ran cold. She put on a turquoise jogging suit—noting that the orange dousing amulet looked nice with it—and went to see if Echo needed anything else. He wasn't in the guest room, but the chicken plate was licked clean. She picked it up and went to put it in the kitchen sink.

She called for Echo and looked through every room, but he wasn't there. As she scanned the living room, she saw that she'd left one of the small side windows open. The screen was dislodged. Echo must have pushed it out and taken off.

Cas left the screen ajar in case the cat came back. She checked the mail, her email, and her voice messages. There was nothing important in any of them, so she made herself a salad and chewed slowly as she thought about the day.

When Cas was a kid, she'd loved fantasy stories, especially after being sent to boarding school. Daydreaming about being a princess or a powerful sorceress helped her pass many hours that she would otherwise have spent bored or anxious. Today, her childhood stories came to life and grabbed Cas by the throat. It had ripped away a veil she'd never expected to see through.

But Cas had to admit that she was a little bit more excited than scared. The council members and others she'd come into contact with seemed to think she had a lot of power. If they were right, she might be able to do some good in the world. Even though she was approaching fifty, maybe the most exciting part of her life was ahead of her.

Cas pondered everything while washing the dishes. When an unexpected sneeze burst out, she immediately braced herself for a wonky magical reaction, but nothing strange happened.

The amulet was working—yippee!

Cas poured a glass of Merlot and headed out the French doors of her dining room onto the deck in the backyard.

When she and Sterling had bought the house, the backyard had been a big part of the reason. Cas had been drawn to it as a natural getaway. Once in it, civilization felt a thousand miles away. There was no fence, but tall hedges grew close enough together to create a natural barrier all around the yard.

Sterling had driven shepherd's hook stakes into the ground periodically along the hedge line. Cas had hung a flower basket on each one and strung white Christmas lights all the way around. She'd worked hard to create five small perennial beds around the yard, and they'd installed a soothing fountain. It was her oasis and the most peaceful place she knew.

Cas wandered around the yard in her bare feet with her glass of wine. She plucked a few dead flowers from a red geranium and then sat on the wooden bench swing near the fire pit to relax. The sky darkened a little as she sat there, and Cas looked up to gaze at the first star that popped out. She took a deep breath and considered what her wish should be. She thought of poor Aunt Petunia. Cas hoped her aunt's house was back in order and Petunia was at peace.

Cas decided that a fire in the pit would be nice. She got a few pieces of newspaper and a lighter from where she'd left them on the table on the deck the day before and dropped them, along with a few pieces from the wood pile and some kindling, next to the fire pit. She got down on her knees and leaned forward to arrange the wood in the pit, but the silver chain that held the amulet around her neck swung forward and got caught on the rough bark. She took the necklace off and put it on the grass next to her so it wouldn't get broken.

She busied herself putting the fire together. When she grabbed the last piece of wood, a beetle ran off it onto her hand. She screeched and tossed the wood back on the ground.

Chaos erupted. The strings of Christmas lights began to dance around in a circle. The hedges groaned and creaked. Then they started moving too—marching along in the opposite direction as the lights.

Every few seconds, a firecracker sound would go off in the yard, accompanied by a flash of colors. A family of six squirrels raced out of the hedges, looked around, and realized they had nowhere to go. They crouched down near Cas and trembled, their eyes wide.

Cas jumped to her feet. "Stop! Be still!" she screeched, but to no avail.

How could she stop this? She looked at her hands. She'd seen other witches make complicated movements with them when they wanted to do something magical, but she had no idea how to do that. When she'd made the iris appear in her hand on the first courser ride, she'd just closed her eyes and thought hard about it. Maybe she could do that—think hard about stopping the madness.

She stood up, clasped her hands tightly together, and squeezed her eyes shut. She tried to envision her backyard calm and back to normal, but her heart pounded and she couldn't get the image right.

A loud pop broke her concentration.

She looked up and had to catch her breath. There, next to the squirrel family, was her new neighbor, Hottie McHotterson. He held a small device in his right hand that

A WITCH TOO LATE

looked a bit like a tuba except it was only around two inches big. It was bright green and had swirly silver markings on it.

Hottie held his right arm and the device straight out from his body and then brought his left hand up to it, pressing on the device's side with his fingers in a fast pattern. The backyard suddenly felt as though a twenty mile-per-hour wind swept through it. Cas pushed hair back from her face, and the squirrel family hunkered down even closer to the ground.

Five seconds passed, and the wind stopped. The hedges and Christmas lights went silent and still. The firecrackers and fireworks ceased.

Hottie brought his arm down and turned toward Cas. "Hi," he said with a smile that made her feel like sitting back down on the ground.

"Hi," she managed to get out. Her throat tried to close around the word.

"I'm Graham Noble." He had the faintest of southern accents and just the right amount of stubble on his cheeks. He switched the strange device to his left hand and held the right hand out to shake.

She took it and tried not to think about how attractive men with strong hands and arms were.

"I'm sorry to just burst in, but it sounded and looked like you could use some help." He walked over to the fire pit, set his device on the ground, and picked up the dampening amulet. "You have to wear this all the time to keep stuff like that from happening until the council figures out another way to help you." He handed her the necklace, and she took it reflexively, putting it on and drawing a deep, calming breath.

"You know about the council? About me?" she asked.

He smiled again. "I'm sorry, ma'am. It was a sneaky thing to do, but the council knew I moved in next to you, so they hired me to keep an eye on you in case you got into something Echo couldn't handle." Graham looked around. The squirrels had disappeared back into the hedges. "Where's Echo?"

"Oh, I don't know. He left the house while I was in the shower earlier. After he had his chicken."

"Hopefully he'll get his tail back here before the council finds that out," Graham said. His lips down-turned slightly. Then he caught sight of the half-built fire in the pit and his face softened again. "Were you building a fire?"

"Yes. That's why I took the amulet off. It's so heavy, and it was interfering with me getting the wood in there. I didn't want to break it."

"Oh, that thing is indestructible. Nothing could break it. Here, let me." Graham finished setting up the logs, placed the newspaper inside them and the kindling on top of that, and lit the paper. Cas went and sat on the swing and watched him. The sky was dark and the moon climbed in the sky.

Once the fire was going well, Graham sat next to Cas and they both watched it for a few minutes. Cas settled down as they sat there, and her pulse slowed to normal.

"So, what brought you to this neighborhood?" She normally didn't pry, but the silence had lasted long enough. Plus, she needed more answers.

"I think you did." He didn't look at her, but she looked at him, surprised. The firelight danced on his face and made him even more handsome.

"Me? What do you mean?"

He finally glanced at her and laughed a little. "I didn't know it was you, but it felt like there was an energy vortex here. And I like those. They're peaceful. Energizing. To supernaturals, anyway—they make humans uncomfortable and antsy. There wasn't any record of a vortex here, but I could feel it. Now that the council told me a little about you, I think you were it—the source of the power. Have you noticed a lot of humans moving out of here lately?"

"Yes! People have been moving both in and out. Mr. Percy and I were just talking about that. Oh, he lives on the other side of my house. Maybe you've already met him? He has a small Westie named Demon he walks several times a day."

"I've seen him, but I haven't formally met him yet."

"He's a character." Cas felt bad that a bit of exasperation entered her voice. She didn't like to gossip, and she didn't think it was right to let on to Graham her feelings about Mr. Percy. A change of subject seemed like the way to go. "You're a supernatural then? Drawn to my energy? Are you a witch?"

He shifted his weight on the swing and angled away from her a tiny bit. "No, I'm no witch."

"I'm sorry. I didn't mean to pry."

Graham laughed, and it was a lovely, full, rumbling sound that emanated from his chest. "I think you have a right to a few questions, since I showed up in your yard with a magical relic, like some kind of Indiana Jones or something."

Cas giggled too. It felt good to laugh about something.

"Okay, like I said, you deserve a few answers. My mother was a witch, but I'm not."

"So you don't have to be a witch if your mother was? I'm still learning all about the rules with the supernatural."

"There aren't a lot of hard and fast rules to it, really. And yes, you can be born non-magical to a magical parent. Two different types of magical beings can also have offspring that are one or the other."

Cas found that interesting. What other types of supernaturals were there? She was pretty sure she'd seen a sprite and a ghost, but they didn't seem like beings that would mate with witches. "But you *are* supernatural, aren't you? Because you were drawn to my energy—what did you call it—vortex? I wonder why I'm an energy vortex."

"I can't say for sure. Maybe it has something to do with your late blossoming. Maybe the strong energy fluctuations around you were a result of that—of your power being dampened for so long."

"Hmm. Maybe." Cas thought about that for a few minutes. The idea seemed strange. Something had been bubbling under her surface for years and she'd been clueless. Cas also picked up on how Graham hadn't answered the question about what kind of supernatural he was, but she wasn't going to push him.

"Again, I'm sorry about being a little sneaky and keeping an eye on you without your knowledge. The council wanted me to keep my affiliation with them under wraps." His brown eyes searched hers.

"I'm not upset. In fact, I'm pretty glad you were here tonight. I don't know how I would have gotten that mess under control. I need to learn more about my power and how to control it. The council tried to send me to my family members who are witches today to get some help. My half-sister and my aunt both sent me away. I have to figure out why I never blossomed properly in the first place."

"Do you have any ideas at all about that?" he asked.

"Well, Aunt Petunia said something cryptic today—she seems to have a touch of dementia and forgets her train of thought—but she said it was a shame I had to suffer for something my mother did."

"Your mother? What did she do?"

"I don't know. She died when I was five, and I didn't even know she was a witch until today."

Graham whistled softly. "That's a lot to take in all at once. You're probably exhausted." He stood up, and Cas felt like pulling him back down. "You should get some rest. My guess is you'll have a busy few days or weeks coming up while you and the council sort things out."

Suddenly, Cas was hit with a wave of pure exhaustion, and the thought of climbing into her big bed upstairs was almost irresistible. As much as she wanted to keep looking at and listening to Graham, she needed sleep. She stood up too. "Thanks again for your help."

Graham smiled and touched the back of her arm. He guided her across the yard and up the deck stairs. "You're welcome. If you need anything, just come over and knock. Anytime. Oh, and keep that amulet on. All the time. That thing is going to be your best friend for a while."

"Okay. I will. I've learned my lesson, I swear."

Graham walked off into the night, and Cas stood there for another moment before heading into the house. She sighed and smiled in anticipation of the nice long, uninterrupted, peaceful sleep coming her way.

Chapter 9

Cas should have known strange dreams would interrupt her sleep. She had been back and forth to the High Court's chamber so many times—of course it would bubble up from her subconscious.

Only the ceiling was visible at the moment, however. She was flat on her back for some reason. Cas' body ached as if she'd run a long distance. Her mind felt sluggish, like she'd had too much wine. She decided the best way to get the dream over with was to get it started. Cas rolled over onto her knees and froze. The dousing amulet that should have been around her neck lay about a foot away from her fingertips. The chain was broken, and the orange stone was shattered into bits along the floor. Two tiny tendrils of smoke rose from the ruins of the amulet. A slight acrid scent filled her nostrils. Her eyes watered, and she brushed at them with a shaking hand.

The murkiness that had been occupying the edges of her mind cleared in an instant. Cas wasn't asleep. This was real. Somehow, she had ended back up in the council chamber. She even still had on the oversized t-shirt and yoga shorts that doubled as her pajamas. But for some reason her old Nikes—the ones she kept in the hall closet—were on her feet. Her heart rate soared. Cas leaped up and spun around in a circle. The room was lit only by the morning light seeping through the chamber's windows.

A WITCH TOO LATE

At first, Cas thought she was alone. But no. There was someone else in the room.

"Archsiren?" Cas took a tentative step forward. "Are you Ok?" About four feet away, in the opposite direction from the smoking husk of the amulet, the witch lay prone on the chamber's floor.

"Archsiren?" Cas whispered but she knew it was useless. The other woman remained silent and staring at the ceiling.

Lavania was dead.

A thin, gray tendril of smoke rose from the body. Cas slapped a hand over her mouth. She hesitated a moment and moved forward, kneeling beside the fallen woman. Cas could see that the smoke rose from a gaping, cauterized hole in Lavania's chest.

"What's going on in here?" Cas snapped her head up. Denzel floated by the door to the hallway.

"I . . . I don't know. I woke up in here and found her." Cas stood up and took a step back from Lavania.

Denzel cried out, "*Terrorem*!" A piercing alarm exploded in the chamber.

Cas covered her ears. She and the ghost stared at each other for thirty seconds before the chamber door swung open, traveling right through Denzel. Valencia, Stu, and Shiloh stood motionless in the doorway for a moment and took in the scene.

Dustin arrived a moment later. Though he was dressed for the office in dress slacks and shirt, his hair was rumpled as if he'd been woken from sleep. He stared at Lavania, then Cas, and his shoulders drooped. "She killed the Archsiren," he whispered.

That seemed to spur the sirens to action. Stu lifted a hand, spread his fingers wide, and jerked them into a fist.

Without warning, Cas couldn't move. It was as if a great vise had gripped her entire body. Her arms and legs wouldn't obey commands. Whatever it was squeezed tighter. It took all her energy to pull in one breath after the other.

She managed to wheeze out a brief defense. "I didn't kill her."

Albert limped past the others and into the room. He went straight to Lavania's body. He used the end of his cane to poke at her before he turned cold eyes toward Cas. "Couldn't help yourself, huh?"

Cas tried to shake her head, but she could only move her neck an inch in either direction. "No..."

"She needs killing. I told Lavania that, and she ignored me. Now she's suffered for it. Go ahead, Stu. Just get it over with. I'm sorry, dear. It's not your fault, but you're too dangerous to live." Albert's brows knitted together, and he leaned on his cane.

Stu shifted his weight from one foot to the other. He licked his bottom lip and rubbed his left palm on his pants. "I don't know. It doesn't seem like the right thing to do, really."

"It isn't right. She's innocent!"

The voice came from the back of the room. Heavy footsteps thudded as more people entered.

Graham Noble, followed closely by a man she didn't know, edged in between Stu and Dustin and came to her side. "Are you okay?" Graham asked.

Cas closed her eyes, feeling a surge of gratefulness.

Graham growled in Stu's face, "She can't breathe. Loosen the binding spell."

The siren's nostrils flared. "You need to watch your tone." He closed one fist and spread his fingers wide, a reverse of the gesture he'd performed before.

Air had never been so sweet. Cas pulled in huge lungfuls as almost everyone in the room watched her with narrowed eyes and furrowed brows. She still couldn't move but was happy to be able to breathe.

Graham touched her shoulder. "Better?"

Cas nodded and the words spilled out. "I didn't kill anyone. I don't know how I got here. I woke up, the amulet was destroyed, and Lavania . . ." Her voice cracked, and she stammered to a stop. She felt something on her foot and managed to direct her eyes downward enough to see Echo.

"Who found them here?" The man who had arrived with Graham and Echo was tall, dark, and decidedly not handsome. His face had four large scars, and one of them extended into his hairline, leaving a two-inch bald spot to the right of the part that went straight down the middle of his head. Before it arrived at his scalp, the scar traveled over his right orbit, and though the eye was still there, it was milky white and fixed, unseeing. He wore blue jeans, cowboy boots, and a beige shirt with a patch that read Crystal Springs Sheriff Department.

"I did, Sheriff Lloyd." Denzel floated near the ceiling above the others in the doorway. "She was kneeling beside the Archsiren's body. I was in the reception area filing some papers when I heard something from this direction. I first thought it was some of the other ghosts engaging in some early Founder's

Day revelry. I thought I'd chase them out and secure the chamber."

Lloyd leaned over Lavania's body and touched her wrist as if testing for a pulse. With the smoking hole in her chest, it was a useless gesture. He straightened and dusted off his hands. "Yep, she's dead. Well, it seems like an open and shut case to me. Witch business, for one, and clear who the murderer is, for two."

Lloyd turned toward Graham and growled at him, "I don't have time for goose chases like this, Noble. Witches can handle their own business."

He glanced at Stu, who still held his hand up to maintain the binding spell on Cas. "Seems like they've got it all figured out already." He walked toward the door.

"I was with Ms. Lorne until just before dawn," Graham pronounced, loud enough for everyone to hear.

That wasn't true. Graham had left well before dawn. Cas flicked her eyes to him but said nothing. She felt a stab of guilt, even though she hadn't told the lie. But Cas thought of Albert's death decree and kept her mouth shut.

The sheriff paused more than half-way to the door. He tossed his head back and let out a few cuss words at the ceiling. Still mumbling under his breath, he took out a notepad and a pencil. "Go on."

Graham volunteered more alibi. "She was having some trouble with gnomes in her backyard. Very destructive bunch. I was over there shooing them out for her."

"And I arrived back at Ms. Lorne's home just after dawn." Echo ignored the sharp looks Denzel and Dustin gave him. The cat had defied orders and now they knew it. "I saw her, unconscious, being taken away in a courser. I didn't see her abductor."

Sheriff Lloyd raised his non-scarred eyebrow at Echo. Cas could feel a sudden pulse in her temple. She was surprised that the sheriff of Crystal Springs knew all about witches and cat familiars. He stared at Echo for another moment before his facial muscles relaxed—as much as they could around the scars—and he shrugged. "Let's see what we have."

He knelt beside Lavania's body and scrutinized every visible inch without moving her. He stood up and walked around in a widening circle, staring at the ground.

"Did this jewelry belong to the deceased?" Lloyd asked, standing by the ruined chain of the amulet.

"No," Albert answered. "That belongs to that woman there. We put it on her to contain her power and look what happened."

"I see a hunk of burned chain. You wanna fill in the facts for me?" The sheriff tilted his head to one side.

Albert huffed. "I wasn't here, so—"

"All right then. Hush up and let me work."

Lloyd knelt by the Archsiren again, touched her hand gently, and checked his wristwatch. The sheriff's left eyebrow shot up again, and he followed it with the rest of his body, rising from the floor to look around at the others. "It's just after 7. The sun came up 'bout an hour ago. She's too cold to have been killed after dawn. Rigor is starting to set."

Shiloh, who had been quiet, gasped and turned away from the body.

Graham said, "It couldn't have been Ms. Lorne, then. Echo and I can attest to the fact she was at home until after dawn."

Dustin cleared his throat. "If I may interrupt. This really is witch business—"

"If it was open and shut, yeah, this here would be witch business. But this don't smell too right to me. The coroner will confirm time of death, but would any of you know why the Archsiren would be here, let's say, before dawn?"

"No, but Lavania did whatever she wanted," Dustin said. "She could've come for any number of reasons or even to work on the Founder's Night celebrations."

Valencia peered down at the body but made an effort to steer clear as she inched toward her chair. "Just last night, Lavania mocked me for not finishing my duties for Founder's Night. She, as usual, bragged about her superiority and how she'd completed all of her tasks. So that's not it."

Dustin's face went still. Then he nodded. "Of course. Our Archsiren was ever vigilant."

Albert cleared his throat. "Now, Sheriff, the problem is larger than you understand."

"Larger than a dead body on the floor?"

The eldest siren's face reddened. "You're not privy to this information, but this woman," he pointed his cane at Cas, "is a menace to our populace at large. She must be dealt with appropriately."

The sheriff turned to square off toe to toe with the other man. "I'm declaring this an official investigation and this woman—what's your name, sweetheart?"

"Cascade. Cascade Lorne."

"Ms. Lorne is under the jurisdiction of the Crystal Springs Sheriff Department. I need her alive until I can button some things up regarding this death."

Dustin shifted from one foot to the other. "Does this mean you're officially opening an investigation, Sheriff? I really don't think that's necessary. See, Ms. Lorne is having a problem with the control of her magic, and unfortunately, Lavania likely got in the way."

Shiloh stepped closer to the sheriff. "Dustin, you aren't a siren. Remember your place. Sheriff, it's true Ms. Lorne is new to our community. And it's true we gave her that amulet as a way to minimize her power. This seems suspicious but after hearing Mr. Noble's information, we'd be happy to cooperate with your department. After all, it would be best for the community, especially with the celebrations so close."

Valencia added, "Though, of course, we'll be looking into this as well." Albert harrumphed. Valencia put a hand on his shoulder and shushed him.

"Why are all of you important types here so early, anyway? I thought witches liked to sleep in," Lloyd said.

Cas noticed the sirens bristled as if the sheriff had insulted them. It was Shiloh who answered. "This is a busy time for us. We had a meeting planned for 7:30 and hoped to begin session at 8."

The sheriff didn't say anything. He folded his arms over his chest and held Cas' eyes as if he read her mind. She could almost see the gears turning in his head.

"As much as I would like to pass this off to you witches, I'll have to take her down and put her in a holding cell. At least until the coroner has a chance to examine the body. Even though you have an alibi for her, Noble, she was still found with the murder victim, and no one else was around."

Her body sagged with the outflow of adrenaline, and if Stu's spell hadn't been holding her up, she would have sank to the floor. The gruff man believed Graham. She wasn't going to be vaporized on the spot.

"I understand, but if the sirens agree, you don't have to take her with you. Maybe you could do something else to keep her secure while you and the council both investigate what happened."

The sheriff tipped his head to the side and waited.

"A leash," Graham said.

A slow smile that looked more like a sneer crept onto Lloyd's disfigured face. "I like that. I like that a lot."

A thin sheen of sweat covered Stu's face. "Pardon me, but there are other considerations that go beyond the help of a leash. Like Ms. Lorne's unfettered magical strength."

The sheriff rolled his eye in the siren's direction. "Yep, that sounds like witch business. I'll leave that to you all as long as she remains unhurt. A leash it is."

"I'm happy about not dying and all, but somebody want to tell me what a leash is?" Cas knew when things were going her way and felt it wise not to interject when it wasn't called for. The help from Graham and Echo was much appreciated. But a leash didn't sound fun.

"It's a magical device invented by witches to keep shifters contained once upon a time. Sort of like a tracker and shock collar rolled into one," Graham explained.

"Yeah, but we've adapted it and now get to use it on non-shifters." Lloyd chuckled. "Like right now."

He pulled what looked like a black leather loop out of his pocket and moved to put it around Cas' neck.

"Sheriff, I think her wrist will work just fine," Graham said.

Lloyd chuckled again and shrugged. He held out his hand and paused. "Oh, that's right, I forgot they got you all bound up." The sheriff adjusted her arm like Cas was a mannequin. He placed the loop over her hand and the thing tightened of its own volition.

It didn't hurt, but it made its presence on her wrist known. Lloyd asked some questions about where Cas lived and worked. After she replied, he used his forefinger's nail to scratch symbols into the leather. Up close, Cas noticed the nail was long, sharp, and curved like a claw.

The symbols glowed glossy ebony and then darkened until they were invisible against the leather.

"There you go, Missy. You can go home and move around Crystal Springs, but if you try to go anywhere else this will alert us, and we'll throw you in a cell. I don't have time to put up with any shenanigans."

Cas tried to nod but couldn't. "Got it."

"Thank Noble. He's the only reason I'm allowing this. It's a witch matter, but laws are laws, and I'm sworn to follow them. Now, if you'll all excuse me, I have more pressing matters to attend to. The Founder's Day parade will be bringing out the party animals, and I have to get my team ready. Deputy Tower here," he waved toward a short man dressed in the sheriff's department uniform, "will secure the scene until the rest of team arrives. Everybody out! Nobody touch nothing."

Stu loosened the spell on Cas so she could walk without help. Dustin led the way to the sirens' private chambers.

The room wasn't as large as Cas expected. Cushioned, high-back office chairs sat around a round conference table.

"I guess we're not killing her," Albert quipped as he eased into a chair.

"No, we can't," Valencia confirmed. "At least right now. But we do have to figure out how to keep everyone around her safe until we can determine what happened here this morning. Obviously, a dousing amulet isn't the answer. That reminds me. We can't afford to let the community find out we resorted to the black market. Dustin, as soon as possible—"

"—I'll take care of it. Discretely," Dustin said. Then added after Graham shot him a look, "Of course, after the sheriff has released it back to the sirens."

Dustin paused before he left the chamber. "Tempeste has arrived in town for the Founder's Day celebrations," he said. "As you know, she has exceptional power—more than any witch in Crystal Springs. Maybe it's providence that she's here. She could perform a more permanent binding spell on Ms. Lorne, strong enough to prevent her from using her powers, knowingly or unknowingly."

The sirens looked back and forth between each other. "Sounds like a good idea to me," Shiloh replied.

"I agree," said Stu. "But someone should get her quickly because I don't think I can hold this spell much longer. Ms. Lorne's power is considerable, and I'm getting tired."

"Very well. Fetch Tempeste for us, Dustin," Albert instructed. "Oh, and don't share what has happened. Let's keep Lavania's death quiet for now."

"Of course," Dustin replied, but Albert, the opportunity for killing having passed, snored in response.

Valencia said, "Stu you're turning colors. You might as well release her. But if she makes a single false move, turn the woman into a frog,"

Stu complied and sighed with relief. He shook out his hands as if they'd cramped.

"Thank you both for helping me," Cas whispered to Echo and Graham after she rubbed feeling back into her fingers. "I woke up here, and I have no memory of getting here or anything that happened. There's no way I could have defended myself against those allegations—I am as clueless about what happened as anyone."

"It's no sweat. I know you didn't kill anyone," Graham said. "Echo came to my house and got me this morning when he saw you being taken away in a courser. We were able to call it back to your house, but it was already empty. Echo took a look at its magical signature and thought it had come here with you. So, we followed it."

"Echo, I owe you big time," Cas said.

"Keep supplying the chicken, Ms. Lorne, and we'll call it even." Echo rubbed his head on Cas' leg, and she smiled down at him.

They waited for about twenty minutes. The sirens all sat down, and they let Cas sit too, after repeated warnings about turning her into an amphibian. Echo took the opportunity to give himself a bath, and Cas wondered where he'd been the night before and what he'd gotten into.

Finally, Dustin opened the chamber door and held it for a tall, gorgeous woman with dark skin, dark eyes, and fluttering purple clothing that sparkled as she walked. It looked sheer, but there were multiple layers, so it was impossible to see through it. Stunning dreadlocks entwined with lavender ribbon reached her lower back, and she had a larger piece of ribbon tied around her head as a headband with long tails. Gigantic silver hoop earrings hung from her ears, and several rings adorned each hand. All the jewelry added sparkle when she moved.

All four sirens stood when she entered. She smiled and waved them back down with a delicate hand. "Peace and blessings to all."

The sirens replied in kind. An intense warm feeling spread over Cas' skin. It was soothing and calm, and she had no doubt it came from the beautiful woman. Was this what immense power felt like?

After a moment, the woman turned her attention to Cas. "Is this her?" she asked.

"Yes," Valencia affirmed. "She blossomed two days ago when someone sent what we think was a perpetuity stone. Unfortunately, we still haven't found it. But she has zero self-control. We need something to quench her power while we investigate some matters. We thought a witch of your skill could be of help."

Tempeste stepped toward Cas. She extended a hand, palm out, and Cas braced for the creepy feeling of being watched by hundreds of eyes she'd experienced when Lavania had used the same gesture. After a minute, she relaxed. Nothing strange happened. Instead she was overcome with the sensation of being wrapped in the arms of a loved one.

Tempeste cocked her head, and her perfectly shaped eyebrows rose a few millimeters. "She is strong," she acknowledged. "Among the strongest I've encountered."

"Can you bind her?" Valencia asked.

"Yes, of course." Tempeste twisted her hands and fingers in a more complicated pattern than Cas had yet seen a witch perform. Once again, all the sensory input coming from the room felt muted, as it had when she'd put the dousing amulet on.

"There. It's done." Tempeste turned her back on Cas and addressed the council. "I hope you figure out who killed poor Lavania—it's a terrible thing to lose such a strong woman." She bowed her head. "Peace to you all. I must take my leave now."

Valencia jumped in her seat, but Shiloh wasn't fazed. "Thank you for your help. We hope to see you at the festivities." Shiloh smiled at the other woman, who smiled back and exited the room.

The minute the door closed behind Tempeste, Valencia snapped, "Dustin told her about Lavania's death after I ordered him not to."

"It's a small town. The sheriff might've told twenty people on his way back to his office. Who knows how she found out?" Stu said.

"Lavania's death creates a problem for all of us—" Valencia started but silenced when Stu put up a hand.

"Later." He tipped his head toward Cas, Graham, and Echo. "Those are matters to discuss among the sirens."

Albert snored so loud he woke himself up. He sputtered and looked around for a moment. His eyes settled on Cas. "Well, you're bound, aren't you? So you can go. We have enough to do around here today. Now we have to deal with poor Lavania—make arrangements."

"That's already done, sir," Dustin said as he re-entered the room. "The coroner will be coming, and the funeral home has also been notified. I know how much this unpleasantness has disturbed everyone. I've arranged for breakfast to be served in the dining hall and pushed the first several appointments to later this morning."

"Ah. That's good. Well, there will be time for a morning nap." Albert used his cane to hoist himself out of the chair. "Check in with those peacekeepers about the stone, will you, my boy? Bring a plate to my private office."

Dustin nodded his assent and left with Albert. The other sirens filed out after them.

Cas flopped into a chair and turned to Graham. "I don't have a good feeling about that sheriff doing much of an investigation into Lavania's murder," she said. "And the council doesn't seem to know where to go next, either. Am I supposed to wait around my house for them to decide I did it after all and either throw me into jail or kill me with a spell?"

Graham sat down as well. "Staying out of the way is smart. I can follow up with the sheriff. He's a good guy as long as you remind him that he is."

"Oh, so I should stake my life on him?" Cas said and rubbed her temples. "Ever since this whole magic thing started, I've been putting my life into someone else's hands or hoping someone would come and save me."

"Well, technically, we did come to the rescue." Echo jumped onto the chair next to Cas.

"Thank you for that reminder, cat."

"No problem," Echo answered and turned his green-gold eyes on her.

"I don't understand half of the things going on. But I'm not waiting around to get blamed for a murder. I'm going to have to do some digging myself," Cas said.

Graham shifted in his seat to face her. "Now, Cascade. You just finished saying you don't understand half of the things going on. The supernatural world is dangerous. Don't tamper with things that might bite."

He was right. Cas' leg bounced as her mind ran through dozens of consequences of playing with fire. Lavania had been murdered, after all. Did she really want to get involved with a supernatural killer?

Cas shook her head. "I'm not going to sit around and wait." She thought about her ex-husband and how much time she'd wasted hoping and praying he'd transform back into her personal hero. "I'll ask around and give a few leads to the sheriff or even the council if I have to. That's it. And you're right. I don't understand this world. I could use a guide. Will you help?"

Graham met her with a stare. He smirked but said, "I'll do what I can. But if I say something is too dangerous, you have to listen. No more incidents like when you took off the amulet."

Cas agreed, and they shook hands. "Echo, what about you? I know you have to report back to the council."

Echo got to all fours and stretched. "The council doesn't need to know everything, and I have nothing else to do at the moment anyway. I'll assist."

They filed into the hallway. "Now we just have to figure out where to dig first," Cas said.

"I couldn't help but overhear your conversation, and I might have an idea." Dustin waited for them in the hallway. He spoke in a hushed tone and moved closer so they could hear him. "The Archsiren did have some enemies."

He looked around and said in a low rush, "If I were you, I'd go to the newspaper offices and talk to the editor." Once the words were out of his mouth, he turned around and went straight to his office without a glance back.

"Well, now we have a place to start," Cas said as she straightened her spine and tried to look brave. "Let's go."

Chapter 10

After a quick stop back home to change out of her pjs, Cas, Graham, and Echo took the courser to the offices of the Crystal Springs Gazette. On the outside, it looked like any normal office. They entered the front doors, and everything looked typical there too. A receptionist sat in the corner. He looked up when they entered.

The nameplate on his desk identified him as Todd. He flashed an amiable smile from a plain but pleasant face. "How can I help you?"

"We'd like to see the editor please," Graham answered.

"Ms. Crossings has a break between appointments right now. I'll see if she's available. Who may I say is inquiring?"

"Graham Noble and Cascade Lorne."

"Ahem."

Cascade started, peered down, and then corrected. "Oh, and Echo the cat."

"One moment, please." The young man crossed the room and entered a door on the other side.

"Ms. Crossings? As in Juniper?" Cas wondered.

"Yes. She's been the editor for a number of years. The town likes her," Graham answered.

"She was my Blossom Greeter," Cas explained.

"She's a nice lady. I don't think she needs the greeter job for the money, but she really enjoys meeting newsprings and welcoming them into the community."

Todd reappeared. "Ms. Crossings is happy to see you now," he announced. "You can go right in." He gestured toward the door he'd entered before and sat back down to answer a ringing phone at his desk.

Graham and Cas entered Juniper's office, and Echo trailed in behind them. Juniper sat at a behemoth of a desk covered with stacks of papers. She scribbled in a notebook as her wild mass of curls bounced. The red glasses slipped down her nose, and she shoved them back up with an irritated jerk.

They waited for her to finish and acknowledge them.

Finally, Juniper sighed and pushed the notebook away. She peered at them over the rims of her glasses. "Oh, Ms. Lorne! It's nice to see you. How are you doing?" She reached both hands out to Cas.

Cas leaned over the desk, took Juniper's hands, and squeezed. "I've been better," she admitted. "Things have happened and I'm in the middle of it, unfortunately."

"Do you mean Lavania's death?"

Cas scratched at her cheek, feeling confused, and glanced back at Graham, uncomfortable. "You know about that?"

"It's a small town, dear. Word spreads quickly. Plus, Sheriff Lloyd has a mouth like a sieve when it comes to witch business."

"I see," Cas said. "So far, I'm a suspect in the Archsiren's murder."

Juniper clucked her tongue. "Terrible business! I've sent someone to the High Court to cover it. Such a shame. How did you get caught up in it, dear?"

"Someone kidnapped me from my home and left me, unconscious, in the council chamber with Lavania. I assume it was the real killer."

Juniper's eyes and mouth both widened. "That's terrible! Of course," she said as she pulled her hands slowly away from Cas, "I have to be impartial. If you're a suspect, I can't treat you differently than any other suspect. We'll report this story fairly."

"I understand. I'm just trying to learn everything I can about Lavania and any enemies she might have had?" Cas inflected her voice to make it a question.

"Oh, well, I wouldn't know about anything like that." Juniper peered down at her desk and shuffled papers around. "I mean, I might, but I can't engage in gossip. Especially with murder suspects."

"Of course not," Graham said.

Cas shot him a "what do you mean" look, and he winked.

He continued, "You're a fair and honest editor. That's why the people here love you. And you know everything about everyone. I bet you could help the sheriff's department with a lot of their mysteries."

Juniper stopped her nervous shuffling and glanced at Graham. "Why, I don't know about that, but I do know a lot of things . . ." Her eyes shifted sideways, landed on a pile of newspapers perched on the corner of the desk, and shifted back to Graham. He continued to smile. Cas, suspecting he was playing at some game, forced a matching expression onto her own face.

Thirty seconds passed in silence. Juniper broke it when she nodded and moved to the pile of papers. She rifled through them for a minute before pulling one out in triumph. "I don't know anything about what you asked me before. But I thought you might enjoy this article. It won an award."

Cas glanced down at the newspaper clipping. A picture of a crumbled, charred building accompanied a paragraph of text.

"I have a lot to do today, but thanks for visiting," Juniper said, ushering them out of her office.

"Thank you for taking the time to talk with us," Cas said, and they moved back into the lobby. Juniper closed her door after them. Cas looked at the clipping again, eager to read the story, but a loud voice caught her attention.

"I want my money back for those ads right now!" The speaker was a huge man who, at first glance, resembled a hairy boulder. His head, neck, and face were covered in shaggy black hair, complete with a long beard and matching mustache. A carpet of hair lined his arms too. He had thick, heavy facial features and stood at least seven feet tall.

"Mr. Barns, I'm sorry to hear that the council declined your permit for the music festival, but I will have to go through the appropriate channels to find out if we can refund you for the ads you purchased from us. If you could fill this out for me, I'll send it to the right department, and you should hear from them in a few days." Todd handed a sheet of paper to the giant man, who snatched it but made no move to comply further.

"T'wasn't the council that declined my permit," he boomed. "T'was only Lavania. She had some beef against me, and she cost me more money than you'll make all year. But I won't have to worry about her when I apply for next year's permit." Mr. Barns grinned, revealing that he was missing quite a few teeth.

"Bear! You shouldn't speak ill of the dead, dear!" A woman Cas hadn't seen stood up from a chair at the edge of the room. "Just fill out the paper and let's go, honey." She was about half the huge man's size, and she had to stand on her tiptoes to put a comforting hand on his shoulder.

Bear Barns looked down at the woman, and his features softened. He snatched a pen from a cup on Todd's desk and bent over to fill out the paper. The woman smiled at him like you would expect a teacher to smile at a mischievous but delightful child.

"Thank you, Mrs. Barns." Todd's voice held relief.

"We should go." Graham put a hand on Cas' elbow and moved her toward the front door of the newspaper office.

When they were out on the sidewalk, they found a bench and sat down to read the clipping Juniper had given them.

The House of Charms in Crystal Springs burned to the ground early this morning, in the absence of witnesses. The owner, Sapphire Caprice, arrived on the scene after the fire department had managed to douse the flames. Quite distraught, she didn't wish to answer this reporter's questions. As a crowd converged, murmurs of a feud between Ms. Caprice and the Archsiren Lavania were heard. Accusations of infidelity on the part of Lavania's husband, encouraged by a charm sold by Ms. Caprice, were bandied about. However, no one would agree to be quoted for this article. It's unclear at this time whether the House of Charms was insured or may be rebuilt.

"It wasn't insured and won't be rebuilt—at least anytime soon," Echo said. "Sapphire was left with nothing, and she had to take work with someone we know."

Cas was puzzled. "Who?"

"Tallulah North," Graham and Echo answered at the same time.

"My half-sister? How strange. Maybe we could find her and ask her some questions."

"Tallulah has an event at the Convention Center today. I saw an advertisement for it on TV yesterday," Graham said. "Sapphire will be there, for sure, helping out."

Cas stood up. "I'm game," she said and grimaced. "Even though I might have to talk to Tallulah."

They took a courser to the Crystal Springs Convention Center. When their feet hit the carpet as the bubble contraption disappeared, they stood in a room about four times the size of a regular broom closet. The walls were lined with shelves that held office and cleaning supplies. "Grab something to take out with you to look inconspicuous," Echo told Cas. "There are bound to be lots of humans milling about. I'm going to blend in with the scenery, but don't worry, I'll stay close."

Cas looked around and decided to take a stapler and some markers. Graham chose a box of pencils. But before they could leave the closet, the door opened, and a woman jumped in. She slammed the door shut and leaned her head back against it. The woman's chest rose and fell, and she closed her eyes.

After a moment, she opened her eyes and straightened up. "I'm sorry to intercede, but I'm trying to meet everyone who arrives by courser and let them know what's going on out there," she said, somewhat out of breath. She was in her mid-thirties and had dark brown hair pulled up in a high pony-tail. Her pink skirt, cream dress shirt, and matching pink jacket appeared custom-tailored. A string of pearls was the perfect match for the cream-colored heels on her feet.

"Oh, hello, Graham. Good to see you. Uh... before you go out there, you should know that there's been some sort of—mix-up." The woman's cheek muscles clenched on the last word, and her hand went to her temple. "I don't know what happened, but two events were scheduled for the same afternoon." She stopped speaking and swallowed hard.

"So it's busy out there? No worries, Gretchen. Thanks for warning us though." Graham stepped forward to move around the pink-clad woman and open the door, but she laid a hand on his arm.

"It's not just any two events. It's one human conference and one magical community event. We never schedule those over each other. It's been a massive headache to keep the humans from noticing all the sprites and brownies."

The way Gretchen continued to rub at her head, Cas thought the headache must be literal as well as figurative. "Sprites and brownies?" she asked.

"Yes. And pixies, fairies, elves, and gnomes. Plus some other small creatures I don't know the names of. Somehow the annual conference of the Association of Diminutive Supernatural Beings was scheduled alongside Ms. Tallulah North's "Get to the Top, No Matter What" talk. And, of course, the ADSB attendees can't contain themselves when humans are around."

"They're playing pranks on people?" Graham chuckled. Gretchen glared at him, and he forced a sympathetic look onto his face.

"Yes. Yes, they are. It's all my staff can do to subdue their constant mayhem and keep the humans happy. We have to blame all their mischief on our building or employees, of course, so it's really making us look bad."

"That's terrible! We came here to find someone, but let us know if we can do anything to help," Cas said. "I'm Cascade, by the way. Nice to meet you."

Gretchen smiled feebly at Cas. "Thank you. Three more hours and Ms. North's event will be over. Then I can focus on figuring out which one of my employees needs to be fired for this debacle. Some days, I hate being the manager." She turned and opened the closet door, her face set in a determined yet pleasant expression. Cas and her friends followed her out into a long hallway.

No sooner had Cas passed through the doorway than an angry shout reached her ears. She turned to follow the sound. A man in a business suit shook his hands and glared at a water fountain in front of him. His clothes were soaked. Gretchen hurried over.

"What happened, sir?" she asked and brushed at his tie without doing much good.

The businessman jerked away. His bald head, which was covered with water droplets, glinted in the hallway lights. "This fountain just went berserk," he shouted. "Nearly drowned me."

Just across from the water fountain, Cas noticed two men dressed in tartan kilts, complete with woolen socks and garters. Both of them fit the term Gretchen had used earlier—diminutive. One guzzled from a red plastic cup while the other attempted to stifle giggles behind his hand. Finally,

A WITCH TOO LATE

he couldn't take it anymore and toppled over onto the carpet amongst peals of uncontrolled laughter.

Gretchen shot the pair a dirty look but focused on the businessman. "Oh, I'm so sorry. I'll get someone to bring you some towels right away." Gretchen reached under her suit jacket and yanked out a walkie-talkie. She moved a few paces away and barked orders into it and then returned to the wet, bald man. "Why don't you come sit down over here, sir? Victor will be here with some towels in a moment."

The man followed along where Gretchen directed him. "You know, I never would have been drinking out of that fountain if there had been proper water in the pitchers in the conference room."

"What do you mean?" Gretchen's eyes widened, and her words came out weak.

"They are all filled with vodka!" he exclaimed. "Everyone's in there right now, drinking it up and having a fine time, but I take medication that reacts with alcohol. I had to find some water to swallow it with, as a matter of fact, and that's when I got soaked. I suppose your people are using the vodka to distract us from everything that's gone wrong at your horrible facility today."

"Um. No, sir. I assure you there must be some mistake. We don't serve vodka during afternoon conferences. Certainly not in self-serve pitchers. Would you please excuse me? Victor will get you taken care of in a jiffy." Gretchen hurried away from the fuming businessman. She walked through large double doors into a massive conference room.

Cas scanned the area for a glimpse of Echo before she and Graham followed, but as promised, the black cat was nowhere to be seen.

The gathering in the room looked nothing like a professional conference. Sport coats were strewn everywhere, lying where they'd been shed. People stood or sat in small groups talking, telling stories, and laughing. Everyone had a glass of clear liquid in their hand. Some people danced, even though there wasn't any music.

As Cas stepped in, she could sense a sort of fever had taken over the room. It had to be more than the vodka. The people in here were too much—their voices too loud, their gestures too manic. This place was about to implode.

On the small stage at the front of the room, Tallulah leaned back against a podium and watched the mayhem with her ankles and arms crossed. The dangerous scowl on her face was fierce. She was dressed in a bright white pant suit with a navy blue shirt and heels. It seemed as if Tallulah had given up on gaining the attention of the audience and was infuriated about it.

Gretchen fluttered around the room and tried to get control of things. Cas intercepted her as she hurried past and whispered a question.

The pink-clad manager nodded. "I suppose that's a good idea. I can have the kitchen witches whip something up in about fifteen minutes. I'm going to get the vodka out of here." Gretchen motioned for several staff members with empty wheeled carts to head over to the table with the pitchers of booze.

Cas maneuvered her way between revelers to the center of the room and climbed up on a table. She banged her stapler and markers together, but they didn't make a loud enough sound. A second later, a piercing whistle echoed through the room from just below Cas, and everyone fell silent and looked her way. "Thanks!" she whispered down to Graham. He winked, which made her heart flutter, and made his way out of the room.

"Hi, everyone! I'm so sorry to interrupt. I just wanted to let you know that there's been a change in plans. We're going to be serving dinner and then dessert with coffee in a few minutes." A happy murmur filled the room.

Cas glanced at her half-sister, who stared back with hooded eyes and a flat expression. "I know it isn't part of the plan, but we know there have been some curve-balls thrown at this event today, and we'd like to make it up to you. So please, finish your drinks and enjoy mingling, and we'll get the food ready. Oh, and don't worry—you won't be missing any of the lecture you paid for. Ms. North is going to make it available as a recording for you. She'll email you the digital files within the next week."

She climbed down from the table and headed for the hallway. There. Dinner and coffee should sober these people up and calm things down. She couldn't suppress a small delighted cackle at the hope Tallulah would have to scramble to create the recording to send to all these people. Cas had to admit, that had been a last-minute ad-lib of pure genius.

Feeling smug, Cas didn't watch where she was going and almost stumbled over something. No, someone. The person in a crumpled heap at her feet was a grown woman, though a tiny one. She was about the size of two-year-old human. But her face said something else—like she was closer to a very mature forty. The woman's horrible scowl didn't match her short tulle skirt and sparkly blue leotard top.

"Just like every other human, aren't you? Think you're the only being in the world worth any space and consideration. Well, pixies are people too! You can't just run over us any time you want like we aren't even there." She got up and put her hands on her hips. Her chin jutted forward as she glared at Cas.

"I'm so sorry! My head was in the clouds, and I wasn't watching where I was going. Pixies are most certainly people! Um. I think." She stuck her hand out. "I'm Cascade Lorne. Pleased to meet you."

The pixie cocked her head and scanned Cas' face as though to determine whether she was really contrite. She finally placed her hand in Cas', which engulfed it. "I'm Sapphire Caprice." Her tone was calmer, but her face still looked angry. She strutted past Cas toward the conference room's exit door.

Cas followed her. What luck that she'd managed to find Sapphire so fast. Now she needed to figure out how to talk to her. "I'm sorry, again. I hope I didn't injure you."

She waved a tiny hand at Cas. "I'm fine. You can go away now. I'm on a break, and you're sucking up my time."

"You work for Tallulah, right?" Cas glanced back at the room of revelers. "She's not having a good day, huh?"

"You got that right, sister. But the law says I get a break and I'm outta here for a half-hour."

Sapphire moved fast, but Cas had no trouble keeping up with her; her stride was easily four times that of the pixie. "Aren't you the owner of the House of Charms? The shop that burned down recently?"

Sapphire stopped short and stared up at Cas. "Yes, I am. Or was. What business is it of yours?"

"None, really. I just recognized you from the stories that ran in the papers, and I wanted to tell you I'm sorry about your store."

Sapphire's fierce look softened a bit. "Thank you," she said, squinting her eyes in suspicion.

"I was wondering if I could ask you a couple of questions about the Archsiren. Did you know she was murdered last night?"

Sapphire sighed and began walking again. Cas jogged a little to catch back up with her.

"Yes, I did. And I don't have anything to say about it. She ruined my life, and I'm not sorry she's dead. But my life's still ruined, so it doesn't matter much," Sapphire said.

"How did she ruin your life?"

The pixie stopped at the doorway to a second conference room. Over her head, Cas could see it was filled with a variety of people who ranged in size from small to tiny. "I don't have the time or desire to talk to you anymore," the pixie said matter-of-factly. "Just watch where you're going with those giant feet, will you? You could kill a Diminutive with them." She spun on her delicate heel and disappeared into the crowd of supernaturals in the conference room.

Cas looked around, unsure whether she should go into the ADSB conference room or head back to the human one. Then she caught a glimpse of Graham near the stage at the front of the room, talking with a small person.

The word leprechaun jumped into her mind when she looked at him, but he didn't resemble the version she had in her mind from St. Patrick's Day cartoons and decorations. Instead of a wizened old, bearded face, he had a smooth, youthful look. His skin wasn't green, and he didn't have on green clothes either. He wore a beat-up black leather jacket and pants with jet black cowboy boots. The guy did have three features that were responsible for evoking the leprechaun term in Cas' mind: red hair—though it was cut and styled in a Mohawk instead of a long, flowing mane—a heavy, square belt buckle, and slightly pointed ears. Cas got an uneasy feeling from him. He gave off shady vibes.

But Graham's presence in the room encouraged her to enter. After all, Lavania's killer could be in this room. In fact, maybe she'd already met her. Sapphire definitely seemed to have a grudge against the former Archsiren.

Cas scanned the room and was shocked to recognize someone else. The small delivery man from SunSprite stumbled her way. The glass in his hand sloshed white contents over onto the floor as he moved.

"Why, hello!" The sprite was tipsy, and his words slurred. His eyes weren't quite focused on her.

Cas smiled at him. "Hello. It's nice to see you," she said.

"Did I see you talking to Sapphire Caprice just now?" he asked.

"Yes. I accidentally knocked her over, and I was just trying to apologize," Cas affirmed.

"Oh, there's no use apologizing to her. She's in a mood that isn't going anywhere anytime soon. Who could blame her, really, after her business burned down and left her with almost nothing? Terrible thing, that." He started to shake his head but stopped when it caused him to stagger to the side. Cas reached a hand out to steady him. He took a gulp from his cup.

"Her business burned down? What was it?" Cas thought she might get some information out of the sprite if she played her cards right.

"The House of Charms. Sapphire specializes in charms and potions. I don't believe the rumors about who did the burning, though, do you? It just doesn't seem like she could really do such a thing." He took another big swallow from his cup.

"Who?" Cas continued to hold onto the sprite's arm to keep him still.

He looked around to see if anyone was close enough to hear and then said in a stage whisper, "The Archsiren."

"Really? Why would she do such a thing?" Cas had to focus to understand everything the drunk sprite said.

"Because she thinks Sapphire sold a charm to a witch who used it to steal her husband. You might know her. That North woman who's famous with the humans." Another gulp.

"Tallulah? Tallulah stole Lavania's husband with a pixie charm?"

"Alledegly . . . I mean, allegorically . . . uh, allegedly. Yes." He took another drink from his cup, and it sloshed more white liquid onto his hand. "Course, the Archsiren couldn't prove it, and she was still trying to find the evidence when someone killed her. She wanted Sapphire to lose her Charms and Potions license on top of losing her business. I don't think she would have rested until she'd totally ruined poor Sapph's life." He shook his head again, and Cas caught him once more.

"Oh dear. That's a sad situation," she murmured. "I'm sorry, sir, but I never caught your name."

"Oh, it's Bixbie. Pleased to meet you. I'm sorry your package was so late. I don't know how that happened. My boss is determined to figure it out, though, don't you worry. Shame when packages get lost like that." Bixbie shook his head, and this time, Cas couldn't save him from falling over. He was asleep before he hit the floor.

Cas knelt down and grabbed the cup out of the sprite's hand before it could tip over. It was odd-looking. White and clumpy. She gave it a sniff and couldn't pull away fast enough. The stuff smelled awful.

"Curdled milk. It's what gets sprites drunk," Graham said from behind her shoulder.

"Yuck." She carried the cup to a garbage can and tossed it in. "I have to find a bathroom to wash my hands now."

"There's one back by the closet where the courser dropped us off. Hey, listen, I have a lead on the river stone that SunSprite delivered to you. I'm going to go see what more I can dig up. Echo can stay with you for now, and I'll see you later, okay?"

"Okay. Thanks, Graham." Cas smiled up at her neighbor and he grinned back.

She didn't have to search for Echo. Soon after Graham left, the cat rubbed against her leg and then took off in a flash of black fur down the hall to the courser closet. As she passed the doorway to Tallulah's convention, Cas glanced in and saw that everyone was seated and eating. That should help sober them up so they could go home. She didn't see her half-sister anymore.

Cas found the women's bathroom and went in to wash the curdled milk off. It was a fancy bathroom with two rooms separated by an open doorway. The initial room was a small lobby complete with full-length mirrors and a small couch with mint green throw cushions. There was a sink and small mirror in one corner. Cas decided to use it instead of continuing on through the doorway into the bigger room that contained the stalls.

"All I'm saying is you could have gone to her and said you didn't buy a charm from me."

"Who needed a charm? Her husband was looking for a way out of his life with her. I didn't need any magic to draw him in. And it was only for a couple of nights before he left town for good."

Cas froze. She recognized both Sapphire's and Tallulah's voice in the next room, and she didn't know whether to stay and listen or flee before being caught. It only took a second to remember that she herself was currently the prime suspect in Lavania's murder. If Cas had any hope of changing that, she needed to figure out who the real killer was. She turned the faucet on and pretended to wash her hands.

"I know that and you know that, Ms. North, but the Archsiren had her own beliefs. She burned down my shop, even though I couldn't prove it, and now I have nothing. And you haven't come forward to help me, so I consider you to be complicit in the ruination of my career!" Sapphire's voice was getting higher and more screechy as she spoke.

"I don't have to listen to this. Your problems with the Archsiren are none of my concern. I took you on as an employee as atonement for something I didn't even do, and I think that's quite enough. Besides, Lavania's gone now, so you'll be able to rebuild your career. Just make sure you keep your mouth shut about what you do as my employee, and I'm sure things will start to look up for you."

Cas knew the conversation was coming to an end and one or both of the women would be coming out into the little lobby in a second. She wouldn't have time to get out the door without being seen, so she sprinted over, opened it, and then let it start to swing shut behind her.

Cas hoped it would look like she'd just come in.

Tallulah came out first and stopped when she saw Cas. She looked her sister up and down.

"Hiya, Lu," Cas said, making an effort to sound casual. "How are you?"

Her half-sister snorted and left without answering. Sapphire followed after a moment. She didn't even glance at Cas.

As she headed out of the bathroom toward the courser closet, Cas thought this trip to the convention center had been pretty interesting. Could Sapphire the pixie have been the one who'd drugged her and taken her to the council's chamber to take the fall for Lavania's murder? It seemed like a tall order—pun intended. Cas wasn't sure yet, but she knew who to talk to next.

Chapter 11

SunSprite Delivery Service was a large metal warehouse with bright orange siding and the neon green SunSprite logo displayed prominently on all four sides. There were twenty or so neon pink vans parked around it that were just like the one Bixbie had been driving when he delivered the stone to her.

Cas and Echo entered through the front doors into a lobby built for people half her size. There were chairs and coffee tables in several areas around the room. Some of them were a typical size she'd expect for adult humans, but others could've fit preschoolers. The long countertop along the back of the room only came up to her thighs. Echo jumped up and rang the bell with his paw.

Cas looked around the large lobby. It was painted the same Pepto-Bismol pink as the delivery vans, with accents of neon green and orange. Certificates of good service and notes from children thanking SunSprite Delivery for giving them tours of the facility lined the walls.

Cas found herself tapping her toe along to the music playing over the speakers. It sounded like a mix of chimes, jingle bells, and cow bells, and an underlying soft drum beat. "That music is quite spritely, isn't it, Echo?" Cas dissolved into giggles at the pun. Even though he couldn't actually roll his eyes, the expression on Echo's face conveyed quite well that he wanted to.

Cas was still smiling when a very small man with black hair shooting straight up from his head stumbled over and leaned on the counter. His eyes were puffy, and Cas wasn't exactly sure what a sprite's normal complexion was like, but she felt pretty confident this one was pale.

"What can I do for you folks?" he asked without making eye contact.

"I was wondering if I could speak with a manager. I have some questions about a delivery that was made to me." Cas eyed the sprite, wondering if he was well.

"A delivery? Made already, you say?"

"Yes."

"Well, what could you possibly have questions about, then?"

"Marvin! You aren't arguing with customers, are you?" A female sprite with white hair in a ponytail appeared next to the first one. She didn't look too hot, either. "I'm sorry, folks, we had a little party earlier, and most of us drank a mite too much spoiled milk. Oh. Please don't tell our boss I said that." Her eyes were red-rimmed, and she blushed with what Cas guessed was embarrassment.

"Don't worry, I won't say a word," Cas reassured her with a smile.

"Thank you." The white-haired sprite looked relieved. "I'm Miriam. Sorry about Marvin; he's grumpy because of a bad headache. Between you and me, he can't handle the hard stuff. Marvin, why don't you drink some water and take a ten-minute break? I'll handle this."

Marvin nodded and headed back through the door he'd come out of, but Cas heard him mutter something about ungrateful customers who couldn't just be happy with their deliveries. Miriam closed her eyes for a moment and took a deep breath. Then she opened them again and smiled brightly. "Now, what were your questions?"

"A package was delivered to me a few days ago, but I think it was late. Like, really late. So, I was just wondering if you could maybe track where it came from and who sent it to me. There wasn't a return address on the box."

"Late? Wait a minute, I've heard about this case. It was Bixbie's delivery, wasn't it?"

Cas nodded.

"I thought so. He wasn't able to come back to work at all this afternoon. He missed the party, but he was at the ADSP conference, and I heard he had a party of his own there. I guess we all got carried away with the milk today. That happens to sprites sometimes. Very festive creatures, we are!"

"That's nice. Festive is good. So, is there any way to track my package?"

"That case is interesting," Miriam said. "Cascade something, right?"

"Lorne, yes, but the package had my maiden name on it. North."

Miriam tapped the keys of a computer on the counter. Cas noticed that her hair and nail color matched—both were the white of egg-shells. Every few moments, the sprite narrowed her eyes or clucked her tongue and then clicked like mad at the keys again. "Yes, quite interesting. That package got lost for about. . . well, that isn't possible." She pecked at the keyboard again. "Hmm. I'm going to have to ask Clark, my supervisor, about this. Why don't you two come on back with me? I'll show you around. Just give everybody a little leeway, if you don't mind. Most of us are feeling the effects of too much of the hard stuff right now."

"Of course. Thank you," Cas said. Miriam opened a swing-out door in the middle of the counter and motioned for Cas to join her. Echo jumped down and followed the women through a large opening in the wall with long slats of heavy plastic hanging down in lieu of a door. They entered a cavernous warehouse, and Cas' eyes and ears were assaulted with wondrous sounds and colors. The music was on full-blast.

Packages of all sizes, shapes, and wrappings floated around the room, some putzing and others zooming at top speed. Sprites were everywhere, manning machines, pushing carts, and loading pink vans backed up to loading docks.

"Here, you'll need this." Miriam handed Cas a helmet. "Watch out for flying packages."

Miriam slapped a hard hat over her own shock of white hair and took off into the chaos, zipping around carts and whizzing past sprites. Cas struggled with the helmet for a few seconds, but it was way too small. She set it back down, took a deep breath, and sprinted after Miriam, Echo on her heels.

There were a couple near misses, but she made it to the other side of the warehouse to stand next to Miriam without getting a head injury or running over any workers. They were in a section of the huge room dominated by shelving, which spanned the space from floor to ceiling. Miriam chatted with a tall sprite holding a clipboard. He was still short enough for Cas to get a good view of the bald patch in the center of his powder blue hair.

"Here she is, Clark," Miriam said. "Bixbie delivered a package to her a few days ago that, according to the computer, has been stuck in our system for thirty-four years."

"Thirty-four years?" Cas and Clark both exclaimed at the same time.

"Yes. I'm sure it can't be right, but..."

"The computers are never wrong, Miriam. You know that." Clark rubbed his temple, and Cas realized he must have a hangover too. How could these people deal with such loud music and fast movements while hung over?

"At least, the computers have never been wrong before. And it's not completely unheard of for a package to be lost for a while. Remember when that Alice Caugherty woman ordered the amaranth-spotted galliwasp from Brazil and it got caught in the loop up between the third and fourth floors? It was there for six months before it finally dropped out onto its proper track. Luckily, it was a long-lived lizard and a magical one to boot, but boy, was it angry. Poor Alice had a hard time calming it down, that's for sure."

Miriam giggled. "Oh yes. I remember Alice's face when I delivered it to her. She didn't remember ordering the poor thing and had no idea what she'd been wanting to do with it."

"Excuse me, please. How exactly do things work around here? I mean, once a package arrives, what happens to it?" Cas asked.

"Oh, when we get a parcel, it's here until it's delivered. It's never out of our hands and doesn't go through a middle man. Every box, envelope, and container entrusted to us is put into a nipper and—"

"Sorry," Cas interrupted. "What's that?"

Clark spun on his heel. "Here, I'll show ya." He crossed to a nearby shelf, opened a box, and withdrew a diaphanous length of fabric about a foot wide. "This is a nipper. Put anything you want inside, and that baby is on lockdown. No magic is getting in or out. Watch." Clark put the material on the concrete floor, dropped his clipboard on top of it, and jumped back.

It was a good thing he'd moved away. The nipper exploded like an inflatable tent. The edges of the material grew ridges like pointed teeth that clamped over the clipboard like a shark swallowing a seal. For a moment, it looked like a large, swollen bladder, but then, with a hiss of air, the thing deflated to form a perfect shrink wrap around its contents.

Clark picked it up and held it out for Cas to inspect. "See? Whatever's inside is on magical lockdown and can't do any mischief." He yanked at the zig-zag seal along one side of the package, but it didn't tear. "Nothing is getting in or out.

"We have to do that because of the large number of magical items we handle, of course. Wouldn't want all kinds of crazy stuff happening in here because package contents went wonky. The drivers have a special device to take the nippers off moments before delivery, and then, whatever's in the package is free to do whatever it is that it does."

"I see. And my package was lost in this warehouse for thirty-four years?"

"Almost, yes. Sorry about that. We'll have to launch an investigation into how it occurred." Clark rubbed his head again and then he yawned.

"I do appreciate your time. I just have one more question. Can you tell me who sent the package?"

Clark and Miriam both stared at Cas as though she'd sprouted a unicorn horn and started prancing around flinging fairy dust. They exchanged a quick glance, and Miriam finally answered, "No, we can't. That's privileged information. You could lodge a complaint and maybe eventually be able to find that out, but it won't be easy or quick. We protect all of our clients, both those who ask us to make deliveries and those to whom we deliver things."

"Of course. I understand. I'll give some thought to lodging the complaint. Thank you so much for your time. Should we see ourselves out?"

"I'll walk you back up to the front," Miriam said. "Clark, are you going to the Founder's Day parade tomorrow night?"

"Right now, all I want to do is sleep for a couple days." In fact, Clark had flopped down on a wooden box, and his eyes were already about seventy-five percent closed. "But I suppose I'll probably be feeling better by tomorrow night."

Miriam and Clark said goodbye, and the white-haired sprite took Cas and Echo back to the front door of the warehouse's lobby. She gave them a pleasant goodbye, sat down, laid her head on the counter, and went to sleep.

Outside again, Cas felt disappointed. "Well, that didn't get me too far."

Echo scratched his ear with a back paw. "Let's take a break and get some dinner. All this sleuthing is making me famished."

"Okay, where should we go?"

Echo said he knew the perfect place, and they took the courser back downtown. It left them in an alley that smelled like a pile of long-dead fish. Cas plugged her nose and jogged out to the sidewalk.

"So where is this place, Echo? Echo?" She looked around when she realized the cat wasn't by her feet, but she couldn't find him. Finally, she peered back into the alley and saw that he was on top of a garbage can, peering in. "Echo!"

He jumped down and ran to her. "I'm so sorry. I have a hard time resisting that lovely smell."

Cas felt her face begin to twist at the thought of eating whatever made the horrible alley odor, and she forced it back into a pleasant expression. She reminded herself that her human sensibilities were different from cats'. Echo didn't seem to be very sensitive, but she didn't want to hurt his feelings. "Can we please just go into the restaurant?" she pleaded.

"Of course. Follow me." Echo pranced down the sidewalk and past a few storefronts before entering a door that was propped open. Cas followed him. She paused to glance at the restaurant's sign: The Cat's Cauldron - Affordable American Food, Casual Dress, Pets Welcome.

Cas had assumed Echo would need to sneak in and that she'd drop food to him under her seat or something. "I've never seen a restaurant where pets other than service animals were allowed. Isn't it a health code violation or something?" Cas glanced down at Echo. "Oh, I'm sorry. No offense."

"None taken. This is a diner for witches and their familiars. That pets welcome business is so humans don't get suspicious if they happen to stumble into the place and see some of us here with our humans."

"Oh! Well, that's nice." They entered and were greeted with a sign that said: Seat yourself. Please clean up after your pet as necessary.

A WITCH TOO LATE

The place had two big dining rooms, and Echo sauntered into the one on the left. He hopped onto the bench seat of a booth, and Cas slid into the opposite side. A waitress was standing at their table before Cas' backside hit the seat. She handed Cas a menu and directed Echo's attention to the tabletop. Under the glass were pictures of various pet-friendly dishes. She pulled out a pen and a notepad and stared at Cas with one eyebrow raised.

"Oh. Okay. Um, what's good here?" Cas asked. She looked up at the waitress, a girl of no more than seventeen with straight, jet-black hair that fell to her mid-back, a long, rather pointed nose, and large but narrowly set eyes. She had a milky complexion marked by acne in several spots. A ring decorated each of her fingers. The name tag pinned to her shirt read Sandy.

"Um. Everything, I guess. I don't know—I don't really eat that much. The fries are good, I think. Maybe the BLT?" Sandy smacked her gum a few times and continued to look at Cas, pen poised.

Cas smiled at the girl. "Okay, I'll take that, then. A BLT with fries. And a chocolate milkshake."

"Yeah. Do you know what you want yet?" Sandy asked Echo. He lifted a delicate black paw and placed it on one of the pictures under the glass on the table. When he removed it, Cas saw that he'd chosen a pâté and sardine platter.

"With a saucer of non-dairy milk on the side, please," he said.

"Sure. Your stuff will be right out." Sandy stuck her notepad in her apron and turned on her heel.

"Very efficient girl," Cas murmured.

"Did you learn anything interesting at our two stops today?" Echo asked.

Cas thought for a minute. "Not too much at SunSprite, but the convention center was interesting." She leaned in close and spoke as softly as she could, confident that Echo's ears could pick up what she said. "That pixie, Sapphire, definitely has a bone to pick with Lavania. She thinks the Archsiren burned down her charms shop, and she's pretty ticked."

Echo cocked his head to the side. "Interesting."

"And I keep thinking about that man at the Gazette. The one who was angry about his music festival permit not being approved. Bear Barns."

Echo nodded slightly. "Yes, he really seemed to dislike Lavania."

The waitress arrived back with the food, set it down, and disappeared again in a flurry of motion.

Cas started to call the lady back to ask for ketchup but then realized she'd left a bottle right in front of her. "Wow. She's kind of amazing."

"Yes, the service here is quite exceptional." Echo dove into his pâté with vigor.

They ate in silence for a while. Cas was hungry, and the food was great. She hadn't had a chocolate milkshake in a long time. Splurging had been a good idea.

The door swung open, making the overhead bell tinkle. Cas recognized Dzovag Livings as he blew into the room like a hurricane. He seemed more disheveled than when she'd seen him outside the council chamber the day before. For some reason, he still sported the same bright orange shirt and tie under the tailored blue suit, but now they were quite wrinkled.

His jowls jiggled as he walked to the counter and barked at Sandy, "Order for Livings."

He surveyed the room with narrowed eyes while the waitress gathered his food. His gaze fell on Cas. Dzovag tossed a few bills on the counter, snatched the bag, and marched straight over to their table.

"I saw you outside the High Court's chamber yesterday. I don't know who you are, but you had better not be taking up all their time with something foolish. Some people in this community have real issues, like me, and the Court is taking its sweet time approving my request. It's ridiculous! Whatever you have going on, I'm sure it's not nearly as important as my business. So learn how to take care of your own problems and get out of my way."

Cas' mouth dropped open. Livings turned and rushed out the door before she could gather her wits. When Sandy dropped off the check, Cas still stared after Dzovag.

"He's an unpleasant man," the waitress said as her eyes followed Cas'.

"What in the world is his problem?" Cas finally found her voice.

"He wants to build a luxury hotel by the hot springs. He says it will bring in lots of money, but of course, most of that money would come from humans. A lot of supernaturals don't want it. Right now, we can manage the humans because we try to keep the hotels and other stuff they like around the outskirts of town. But this hotel would be smack dab in the middle of it," Sandy explained.

"And near the hot springs, which is a haven for many of us," Echo added.

"I see. Well, he sure seems adamant about getting it built."

"It's all he's been talking about for weeks. I'll take the check up for you when you're ready." Sandy wandered away to check on a man and his Rottweiler on the other side of the dining room.

"Hmm. Livings and Lavania sure seemed to be angry with each other yesterday," Cas said.

"Yes, they were. He seemed to believe the Archsiren might stand in the way of his hotel," Echo agreed.

"Well, I'd say he's suspect number three. So Sapphire, Bear, and Dzovag. Quite the motley crew of potential killers. And I have no idea how to narrow it down from here." Cas sighed.

Without warning, Cas had the spine-tingling feeling that she was being watched. The hairs stood up on her arms, and she scanned the room. She happened to glance out the window. And that's when Cas spotted her: the auburn-haired lady who had been following her stood on the sidewalk, watching. But the second their eyes met, the other woman looked away and hurried off down the sidewalk.

Cas tossed some cash on the table and sprinted out of the restaurant. She caught a glimpse of auburn hair as the mystery woman turned the corner at the end of the block.

Cas jogged to the corner but slowed down to peek around. The woman's footsteps were silent as she retreated down the sidewalk. She glanced over her shoulder at Cas but kept moving.

"Wait!" Cas cried out. "Who are you?"

But the woman said nothing and continued on. Cas followed, intent on finding out who this person was once and for all. The woman made a quick left into the fish-scented alley, and Cas followed, sure she'd be able to catch her. But the woman moved full speed forward, even though she headed toward a brick wall blocking the end of the alley.

"Hey," Cas called when the woman couldn't go any further. "I just want to talk."

But the woman didn't slow down when she arrived at the wall. She went through it. Just like the door to the council chamber had gone right through Denzel that morning.

The mystery woman who'd been following Cas all over town, was a ghost.

Chapter 12

They decided to call it a night and went back to Cas' house for some rest. Echo dashed off right away, headed for the guest room. Cas made a circuit through the house and checked all the windows, making sure they were shut tight. She hoped that would keep the cat safe and inside so he wouldn't get into trouble with the council. Though Cas suspected it may be futile. If Echo wanted to break out, he would.

Cas got a glass of wine and settled into her favorite chair in the living room with a book. She loved reading mysteries. Before all the craziness started, she'd checked out this new one from the library. Maybe reading it would help her get into the right mindset to solve her own mystery.

No sooner had she cracked the book open than a loud banging made her jump. Someone was pounding on her front door. Cas jumped up and clutched the book to her chest. Echo came racing down the stairs, and they crossed to the door together.

Mr. Percy stood on her front stoop. He was thin, haggard, and his face had purple bruises all over it. Her neighbor's left eye was almost swollen shut, and a split lip completed the gruesome picture.

Cas covered her mouth to keep from yelping. Then she noticed Graham standing behind the beat-up man. He gave Percy a little shove, and Cas moved aside to let them both in.

She pulled out a kitchen chair for Mr. Percy. "What happened?" Her gaze moved to Graham's face. "Did you do this?"

"No, it wasn't me, but I probably would have if I'd gotten to him first." Graham's voice was almost a growl. It sounded as if anger broiled beneath the surface. Percy's gaze dropped to his folded hands, and he didn't say anything.

Cas looked from one man to the other and back again. "I don't understand. What's going on?"

Graham pulled out a chair and sat down behind Mr. Percy. Cas noticed he stayed close enough to grab the smaller man if necessary. "While we were at the ADSB convention," Graham said, "I ran into a guy I know as a casual acquaintance. He's a leprechaun who has some superficial dealings in black market magical items. Name's Seamus Cartwright. I got to talking to him, and it turns out he'd heard about a perpetuity stone showing up on the street and disappearing again. No one he knows actually saw it, but the word among the dealers was that an incubus had it."

"Incubus?" Cas' stomach pitched. Something else supernatural. She'd heard the word before but didn't know what it meant in the context of her new life. Forty-eight hours ago, witches had seemed like make-believe.

"A being that feeds off the life force of others. They'll siphon from humans but prefer magical energy from supernaturals." Graham sounded disgusted, like the words coming out of his own mouth were dirty. Percy's head hung a little lower.

"So, an incubus stole my river stone?"

"It's more than a common rock. A perpetuity stone is an artifact that can hold and channel the entirety of a person's magical power. The stories say that, long ago, witches used them against their enemies. The stones in existence were outlawed and assumed to have been destroyed. And, yes, an incubus stole yours. That incubus." Graham jerked his thumb toward Mr. Percy.

Cas' eyes widened. "He's an incubus?"

"Yep. I had a hunch about it when I saw him a few times around the neighborhood. Sometimes he was plump and healthy, like a tick, and other times, skinny and sickly. That's pretty common with incubi—they look robust after eating and later horrible as it wears off and they get hungry again. When Seamus mentioned an incubus, I thought of Percy as a likely suspect since he lives right next door. When I went to ask him some questions, I could see somebody else got to him first."

"I didn't do anything! What right do you have to detain and question me?"

"Not much right at all, I guess. I'll be calling the sheriff to take over soon. But I thought we'd come over here and have a little chat with Cas first, since you've been feeding off her for years."

Cas dropped her book. Echo dodged in time to avoid it falling smack on top of his head.

"I didn't do anything wrong!" Percy shouted and jumped up from his chair. Graham shoved the incubus back down.

"Well, I didn't," he grumbled in a more subdued tone. "I never took more than necessary and only when Cascade was putting off excess. Her energy was never consistent, and when I did feed, it was a tiny amount. I made sure to be careful."

A light bulb went on in Cas' head. This is why Mr. Percy had always found some excuse to touch her; he was taking energy. Feeding on her. Cas' whole body shivered. She thought of all the times throughout the years he had betrayed her trust.

Percy must've read Cas' body language because his face crumpled. He studied his hands again. "I'm sorry," he said. "It's what I am. I have to eat to live, just like everyone else. I can't change how I do that."

"So what happened the night Cas blossomed?" Graham interjected.

Still looking down, Percy sighed. He replied in a clear voice, but he sounded miserable. "I felt a surge of power from your house, Cassie. I was drawn to it—it was impossible to stay away. When I got here, you were unconscious. I checked your pulse and it seemed fine. The energy—the power coming off you—was massive. I'd never experienced anything like it before. I couldn't resist and uh..." He cast a sidelong glance at Graham. "I fed. But just enough to curb my cravings. I would've never hurt you. Then I noticed the stone. I could feel something emanating from it, like a residue. So I grabbed it and left. I knew it must be magical, and I figured I could sell it. I've been experiencing a lull in freelancing gigs lately."

"So you fed from an unconscious woman and stole her property for your own financial gain." Graham's voice shook a tiny bit with restrained fury.

"I didn't hurt her. I'd never hurt her. And I didn't gain anything financially because I didn't sell the stone."

Graham's eyes widened. "What? You still have it?"

"No. I didn't sell it because someone stole it from me before I could. They're the ones who did this." He pointed at his own busted-up face.

Graham stood up and moved so he could face Percy. "Someone took the stone from you?"

"That's what I said. I tried to say that before you dragged me over here."

"Who was it?"

"I don't know. They didn't feel like witches. Their energy, I mean. They could've been human far as I could tell. But whoever it was came up on me quick and I didn't have a chance." Percy pouted like a child.

Graham and Cas exchanged glances. Cas wondered if he was thinking the same thing she was: maybe Lavania's killer was the one who'd beaten up Mr. Percy and stolen the perpetuity stone. But could they have been ordinary humans?

"I'm calling the sheriff," Graham said with a final shake of his head. He pulled out a cell phone and moved to the other side of the room, but his eyes never left Mr. Percy. After he talked for a minute, he put his phone away and returned. "Sheriff's busy, but he's sending Deputy Chris Wave over."

Cas didn't know what to do with herself while they waited, so she made some tea. She prepared a cup for herself and Graham. Percy sat quiet and forlorn. The idea that he'd been feeding off her made Cas' skin crawl.

Despite her misgivings, her instincts made her think Percy was alone in the world. Sort of like Cas herself. She pulled a package of frozen peas out of the freezer and tossed it on the table in front of Percy. He nodded a thanks and slapped it over his eye. She filled a shallow bowl halfway with non-dairy milk and put it on the floor for Echo.

An awkward silence settled on the room. Cas' mind raced as she tried to integrate this new information about Mr. Percy into everything else she'd learned in the past couple of days.

Graham answered the door when the deputy knocked and let the young man in. He was about six feet tall and so thin that Cas thought he'd be invisible if he turned sideways. He had a well-shaped goatee and bicep muscles that threatened to tear his short-sleeve shirt's arms wide open. The corners of his mouth turned downward, and his eyes narrowed. "Why am I here?" He had a stone-cold voice to match his cold, chiseled features.

"This incubus stole a magical artifact from Ms. Lorne here. Tried to sell it on the black market. But some Big Bad roughed him up and stole it first." Graham adjusted his stance so he was squared up with the surly deputy. It reminded Cas of how two male dogs might posture and size each other up. "The artifact is dangerous, and the council is searching for it. I figured Sheriff Lloyd would want to take him down for questioning."

"You thought wrong, Noble," the younger man growled. "He's busy with matters that are actually important. Witch business isn't his priority. You guys need to wait for him to check in on you and the council, not vice versa."

The unpleasant man turned his attention to Cas. She straightened her spine and returned his gaze without flinching. Her heart was doing quite a dance, but she refused to be intimidated.

"What about you, lady? Have you been trying to play amateur sleuth and save your own skin?"

Cas felt her jaw clench and took a breath before answering. "I didn't kill Lavania, and your office doesn't seem too interested in figuring out who did, so I am asking a few questions here and there, yes."

Wave took a step toward Cas. It took all her resolve not to move backward. Graham took a discreet step sideways so he stood in front of her. The deputy smiled and revealed sharp, shiny teeth. "Oh, I see," he said.

Graham crossed his arms, inclined his head, and said nothing.

"Well, I'll tell you this, lady. You're not a detective, so you shouldn't be playing one in your spare time. You keep sticking your nose in where it shouldn't be, and you're going to be in way more trouble than you already are." Wave jabbed a finger at her as he snarled the last words.

"That's enough, Chris. You don't have a right to threaten her. She's cooperating with both the sheriff's and the council's investigations. How about you focus on your job, which, right now, is dealing with Mr. Percy here."

"More witch problems. Listen, Noble. I know you have some pull with the sheriff. For some reason, he seems to like and respect you. But I'm telling you right now—you'd better watch your step. The rest of us in the department don't care about your opinion as much, and Lloyd doesn't want to be yanked into witch business, anyway. That little witch behind you is trouble with a capital T. You'd do best to walk away and find another tail to chase."

Cas opened her mouth to protest but before any words came out, Graham growled low in his throat and stepped forward until his chest was only an inch away from Deputy

Wave's. "Listen, son," he said through clenched teeth. "If you're not going to do your job and question Percy, I think you'd better be on your way. You've about worn out your welcome here, and I don't want to have to get my clothes dirty putting a pup in his place tonight." He hesitated and moved a fraction of an inch closer to the younger man. "But I will."

Cas drew in a sharp breath. She watched as Wave's right hand slowly clenched into a fist. His arm drew back a tiny bit but hesitated. The air was thick with the tension of unshed violence. Cas was afraid the deputy would strike but knew it would be silly to get in between the two men.

Wave took a deep breath, relaxed his hand, and leaned back from Graham. "Hey, you don't have to take my advice, old man. No skin off my nose. But I don't have any work to do here. Let the witches deal with the incubus. And when the sheriff's ready to address your girlfriend's case, he'll contact the council. Not the other way around." He turned and walked out the front door, closing it behind himself. Cas heard his car's engine fire up and fade away as he backed out of her driveway.

Graham cracked his neck and turned to Cas. "Are you okay?"

"Yes. Thank you."

"The kid's got an attitude. Somebody'll pound it out of him someday."

"I'm glad it wasn't you doing it today in my kitchen." Cas smiled and Graham laughed. She liked how it sounded joyful and masculine all wrapped up in one. Cas couldn't help but like how he'd stepped up to her defense. Graham being all assertive was sort of... sexy.

A flush rose up Cas' neck and she willed her body to behave itself. She glanced up to see Graham watching. Their eyes met and held for a second too long. Cas broke the stare first and cleared her throat. Graham covered his mouth to suppress a soft cough. They both looked at Mr. Percy.

"All right, man, I guess you're released on your own recognizance for now," Graham said to the forlorn incubus. "We'll talk to the council about this tomorrow, and I'm sure they'll send a squad out to ask you some questions."

Percy's shoulders sagged as if they'd been relieved of a great weight. He nodded, stood, handed Cas the package of peas, now only cool, and walked to the front door. Mr. Percy stopped with his hand on the knob and turned back toward Cas. "I'm sorry, you know. It's not my choice to be like this. I really didn't ever want to hurt you. I like you and so does Demon."

Cas swallowed hard. She felt a little bad for her neighbor, but she was still too creeped out by the whole energy eating thing to really forgive him yet, so she said nothing.

"Make sure you don't go anywhere," Graham reminded him.

"I don't have anywhere to go." Percy let himself out.

"Well, that was interesting," Echo said. Sometime during the exchange, the cat had polished off the evening's refreshment. He bathed the milk off his face and stretched each leg out one by one before heading back toward the stairs. "Another piece of the puzzle solved but more pieces introduced. I'm going to take a long nap and see if that helps any of those pieces snap into place."

"That's a great idea," Graham said. "I'll come get you both in the morning, and we'll let the High Court know about Percy." He moved to the door and Cas followed him.

"Thanks again. You and Echo are priceless."

"All in a day's work." Graham grinned, and his dimple made Cas' stomach jump a little.

She closed the door behind her neighbor, locked it, and checked all the other doors in the house before she went up to bed. She had a fitful sleep filled with dreams of a crocodile with Percy's face trying to eat her. She didn't fall into a restful, dreamless sleep until close to dawn and slept in until nearly 11:00 the next morning.

She took a shower, got dressed in jeans and a baby blue cotton knit shirt with short sleeves and a scoop neck, and put on a little make-up. When she arrived downstairs, Echo was already in the kitchen. He sat in a sunny spot with his eyes half closed.

"Good morning!" Cas said brightly to the cat. "What would you like for breakfast?"

"Good morning," he answered with a yawn. "Do you have any sliced turkey breast?"

Cas opened the refrigerator door and hunted around a little. "I only have low-sodium ham," she said as she glanced over her shoulder at Echo. "But I could spread some cream cheese on it."

"Delightful. Thank you."

Cas busied herself with Echo's food and brewed a fresh pot of coffee. Graham knocked on the door a short while later, and she let him in. He carried a brown paper bag over and set it on the table. "Mornin'," he said. "I brought bagels. You sure slept in. I've been watching for signs of life over here since 9 am."

"I know. I had trouble falling asleep. Would you like a cup of coffee?"

"That sounds great. Black, please." Graham sat down at the table. A cheerful silence fell over the room as they all enjoyed their late breakfast. As stressful as the past few days had been, Cas realized they'd also been really good. She'd gained two new friends, and that was nothing to sneeze at.

Once everyone was full and the dishes were in the sink, Echo called a courser and they took it to the Courthouse. Cas noticed there were not as many people milling about in the lobby as usual, and she mentioned it to her companions.

"Tomorrow's the big Founder's Day parade," Graham explained. "Most people take a couple of days off to prepare. The Court will only see cases it absolutely has to today and tomorrow. The sirens usually spend this time schmoozing with out-of-town witches and such. They might not even be here."

When they got up to the council's reception area, Waverly was there with her purse in hand and was heading for the door. "You all might as well sleep here for as often as you've been around lately," she said.

"We have to report a development in Cas' case to the Court," Graham told her with a smile that did nothing to move Waverly's bored features.

"They're not here, but Dustin's around. I guess I can page him for you before I leave."

"Thanks, we'd appreciate that." Cas delivered her brightest smile. It was kind of a fun challenge, trying to get Waverly to show some interest in something.

The blue-haired receptionist paged Dustin to the lobby and left.

They waited for at least ten minutes before Dustin entered the room and greeted them with a warm smile. "How can I help you this morning?"

"We have a lead on the perpetuity stone," Cas said. "Graham did some digging and found out that one of my neighbors, Mr. Percy, is an incubus who's been . . ." She stopped for a minute and swallowed hard. She was still having trouble digesting this. ". . . feeding on my energy for a while. He admitted to coming into my house when I was unconscious after the river stone arrived. He took it and tried to sell it on the magical black market, but someone caught up to him first, beat him up, and took the stone."

Dustin's eyes widened. "Wow, that's a big lead! The sirens are all out right now, but I'll send a peacekeeper squad to talk to this Percy character."

Denzel floated through the wall and handed a piece of paper to Dustin. He reminded Cas of the ghost woman who'd been following her. "Dustin, did you know my mom?" she asked suddenly.

"Oceane?" Dustin studied the paper in his hand. "I was only a teenager, but I knew of her. She had a penchant for getting into trouble sometimes. Dabbling in magic best left alone." He seemed to realize he shouldn't speak ill of Cas' deceased mom and looked up from his paper. "She was beautiful, Ms. Lorne, and always extraordinarily kind to me whenever our paths did cross. My dad had dealings with her from time to time, of course, and even though she was troublesome for him, he liked her too."

"Your dad?"

Dustin's jaw muscles clenched a fraction. "Yes. He was a shifter in the sheriff's department. Died a while back."

Cas paused for a moment in respect for Dustin's father. She ventured to ask the question she'd been leading up to. "Do you know if my mom is a ghost?"

Everyone's gaze swung to Cas. She felt herself shrink under the scrutiny. "It's that I've seen some of them around town, and I wondered if all witches become ghosts."

Dustin shook his head. "No, they need a license for that, among other things. It's actually quite complicated. Denzel, would you please fetch me the Undead Directory from the council chamber?"

Denzel left in a flash and returned with a book, which he handed to Dustin. The council assistant paged through it until he got to the right section. He used his finger to trace down the page. "Ah, here she is: Oceane North. No, she isn't a ghost. She's buried and at rest in the Crystal Springs cemetery, though."

He snapped the book shut and handed it back to Denzel, who floated through the wall with it. Cas wondered if Denzel could aid the passage of any solid object through another.

She decided that was a question for another time. She turned to Graham. "I'd like to go to the cemetery and visit my mom. I haven't been to her grave since I was a kid."

"Mr. Noble," Dustin interjected. "Sheriff Lloyd called me this morning. One of his deputies had been in his office yelling about witches and their friends early in the day. He said that he and the rest of the shifters in his department are getting increasingly irritated with being called on to handle witch business. The Founder's Day celebration isn't doing anything to relieve those feelings. Perhaps you could head to the sheriff's office and help them all calm down? You're a true friend to the witch community, and you truly have Sheriff Lloyd's ear."

Graham nodded. They thanked Dustin and left. They made their way to the hover pad and descended to the main lobby, which they crossed in silence.

Graham stopped at the courser pad. "Cas, don't stay at the cemetery too long," he warned. "The gates are warded to keep the unlicensed undead in, and they close at dark. The newly deceased can be somewhat unpredictable."

Cas glanced outside. It was still early afternoon, so she had plenty of time.

"I can take you to the cemetery, but I'll need to wait outside for you," Echo said. "I'm really not comfortable in there."

"That's fine, Echo. I understand." Cas nodded, grateful that her friend would be nearby, at least. Cemeteries were creepy, but she felt an incredible drive to go see her mom.

Chapter 13

The cemetery was huge and beautiful. Manicured, fern-green lawns stretched so far, Cas couldn't see where they stopped. Echo stopped and sat just outside of the majestic wrought-iron gates. The entrance was made of two halves that swung outward from each other. The sides had symmetrical intricate, scrolling designs welded into them. They were wide open, inviting visitors to enter the calm space within.

"I'll just be under that shrub napping," Echo said with a yawn.

"Thanks. I shouldn't be long."

Dustin had given Cas a slip of paper listing the section of the cemetery her mom was buried in, and Cas wandered in that direction. It was the perfect day: blue sky with a few cottony clouds, a light breeze, and seventy degrees. Fall was on its way, and a few leaves were beginning to change.

As Cas walked, she looked around at the grave sites and could tell this was an old cemetery. Some areas contained tiny headstones with names eroded away by time. In other sections, there were huge, majestic stones with poems etched in beautiful lettering, plaques placed flush with the ground, simple crosses, and even a few big mausoleums. A small creek meandered its way through the cemetery, and some areas were quite wooded while others were flat and grassy. Cas thought the place looked like it covered at least twenty acres.

She checked her slip of paper and made a slight course adjustment, heading inward toward the creek. Movement caught her eye. An auburn-haired woman knelt by a headstone, brushing it off with a feather duster.

No. It couldn't be. Cas power-walked another ten feet. As she got closer, there was no doubt. It was her. The woman who'd been following her.

This time, there was nowhere to run. Cas was going to find out why the woman was stalking her once and for all.

Yet, unlike the other times, the mystery woman seemed unaware of Cascade. She hummed while plucking weeds from around a headstone. It was only when Cas was within five feet the woman glanced her way.

Cas froze, ready for anything. But the mystery lady just gave a small smile and re-focused on her work. There hadn't been an ounce of recognition in her eyes.

"Um. Hi." Cas relaxed out of her battle-stance. "I'm Cas."

"Oh. Okay. Hi there. I'm Violette." She waved a hand without looking up.

Cas almost waved back. Almost. Violette wore a sleeveless yellow sundress. She looked older than Cas would've guessed. Silver streaked the auburn hair and a few fine wrinkles lined her face. Maybe Violette was in her mid to late sixties.

But Cas scolded herself to snap out of it. She attempted to look stern by rolling her shoulders back and lifting her head a little. "Why have you been following me?" She spat the words out before losing her nerve.

"What?" The other woman stood up, feather duster in hand. Her eyebrows knitted together as she pouted a little.

"You were at The Cat's Cauldron last night, watching me eat with my cat. I mean, my Echo . . . my familiar." Cas felt flustered by Violette's confusion. It didn't seem feigned at all.

"I wasn't at that diner last night, and I don't follow people." Violette appeared sincerely troubled. She studied Cas' face. "Wait, what did you say your name was?"

But Cas didn't have the opportunity to answer.

The other woman jumped as if she'd been stung by a wasp. Her face smoothed out, but she said, "Oh dear. You have me confused with someone else. I need to go now. Have a good evening." Violette scooped up the feather duster and other supplies. In the next instant, she hurried off, with furtive glances over her shoulder.

Now it was Cas who stood with eyebrows furrowed. That was strange. Violette didn't seem to recognize her, but there was no question that had been the woman who'd been following her. Cas considered chasing her down and demanding more information. But the sun was getting lower in the sky. Graham's admonition about not staying in the cemetery too late rang in her ears. She'd wasted more time than she'd meant to meandering her way through the gravesites enjoying the lovely weather. If she let Violette go, there would be time to visit her mother's grave. Cas decided to learn more about the strange woman later.

She glanced at the paper scrap and realized her mom's gravesite was close. In fact, it was only a few yards away.

The headstone marking her mom's grave stood about three feet tall. It read:

Oceane (Lovebrooke) North
~ Wife, Mother, Friend~

A WITCH TOO LATE

~ Sweetness and Spice ~

~ Virtue and Vice ~

Gone Too Soon: A Light Too Bright for This World

The site was tidy, and a small pot of white and purple pansies sat near the stone. Cas dipped her finger into the soil. It was moist. Who was taking care of her mother's gravesite?

Cas sat down next to the stone and gazed at it for a while. She recalled the few memories she had of her mom. Oceane had always been laughing, rarely acted stern, and there had never been a time when she wasn't ready to run, twirl, skip, and play games with Cascade. She'd been a good mom.

Aunt Petunia's words floated into Cas' thoughts. *It was a shame what your mother did to you.* What had her aunt meant? But Petunia's word was less than reliable. Still, could whatever she'd meant be related to Cas' situation now? She wondered again what her mother had done. Dustin had mentioned her mother being mischievous too. Maybe she'd ask him about it again and get more specific information.

Cas didn't know how long she sat there. But when she came out of her thoughts with a start, the sun had dipped low in the sky, casting long shadows across the cemetery. The trees and greenery had the special golden glow they get just before sundown.

Cas jumped up and retraced her steps. She paused at the gravesite that Violette had tended. The headstone read:

Violaine Mizzle

A Beautiful Soul with So Much to Give

Next to Violaine's headstone stood another identical one, but it wasn't complete. The death year hadn't been added yet. The plot was for someone intended to be buried next to

Violaine. Cas shivered when she read the name: *Violette Mizzle*. It was creepy to have just met the person who would lie there someday. She reread the dates on the tombstones. The birthdate was the same. Violette and Violaine were sisters. Twins.

A sharp clanging rang out across the cemetery, snapping Cas back to the present. She peered into the distance. *Oh no!* The cemetery gates were closed. She had to get out of there. She began to power-walk, dodging headstones. It wasn't dark yet. Graham must have been wrong about when the gates closed. Well, nothing bad would happen before dark, right?

Cas really didn't want to find out. She sped up and finally made it to the edge of the property, where there was a straight line of unimpeded grass. The sun had dropped below the tree line now. One side of the cemetery was plunged into dusk. The western side still retained the last dregs of the day's light.

Okay, the gate wasn't far now. It didn't look too high to climb. Graham's warning looped in her head. Cas scolded herself for dilly-dallying and kicked her speed up another notch.

Something wet, cold, and clammy brushed past her arm. She screeched and dove away from it. But the move made her stumble. Cas braced the fall with her hands and scrambled to turn over.

Above her hovered a creature of nightmares.

It possessed a grotesque likeness to a human but more resembled a skeleton covered in muscle, without fat or skin. Pallid strips of grey flesh hung from its face like morbid jowls. And its mouth was a gaping maw of the deepest pitch—an abyss so craven—it seemed as if it could suck up the colors from the world around it. The legs and feet protruded from tattered colorless trousers.

Cas inched away. But the thing responded by opening its hideous mouth and cackling. The sound was enough to slap Cas back to herself. She lurched to her feet and ran. The thing gave chase. Cas could feel the bitter coldness of its fingers straining for her neck.

It lunged. Cas stopped short, letting it sail by. The creature slammed with a bone-crushing smack against an upright headstone.

Not that it mattered. The horror sprung back up as if nothing had happened. Two more skeletal shapes joined the first, and one by one, they took turns snapping cavernous jaws and reaching for Cas with desiccated, boney fingers.

Cas dodged, weaved, and bobbed. She sucked in painful gasps of air, but about a hundred yards from the gate, a cramp almost bowed her over. The beasts had their opening. They attacked. Cas stumbled and fell to her knees.

A blow to the back of the head sent her down the rest of the way. Cas flipped over and flung an arm up. She felt the strike, but an ice-cold agony exploded in her arm seconds later.

They towered over her, cackling. One croaked in an unearthly voice, "When do we get to eat her?"

Cas cradled her injured arm and scooted backward until she was against a headstone. A white slash puckered the skin along her arm. Frozen beads of blood decorated the wound. The sheriff's leash still hung around her wrist but dangled by a thread. Cas snapped it and tossed the thing at her pursuers' feet.

"I don't see why we have to wait. Let's eat her now," a second creature answered.

No, you're not. After all this, Cas wasn't gonna let herself get eaten. She used the headstone to push to her feet.

"Cascade!" It was Echo. He perched on a fence to her left. "You have to run. NOW!"

One of the things jabbed a skeletal finger in his direction. "Shut your mouth, cat, or you're next!"

It was only a second of distraction, but Cas took it. She edged past the closest one. The creature made a wide, wild swing but only managed to clip her upper arm.

The pain was more immediate this time. Cas ran, but she didn't know where to go. The gate loomed ahead, but she could hear the cackles of the creatures behind her.

Echo hissed and leaped from the top of fence. He angled toward Cas at a sprint. "Protect yourself!"

Cas heard the warning. But how? Her legs pumped. Up ahead, she could see a thick chain connecting the two halves of the cemetery's gate. It was massive, and, in an instant, a picture of it sprang to her mind. She could feel it, taste the metal in her mouth.

Behind her, she heard a hiss and a screech as Echo threw himself at the beasts. He leapt from one to another, scratching and biting as the things screamed.

"Okay, okay. Help Echo, Cas. Help him." She stopped about five feet from the fence line. She took the image of chains in her mind and pushed at it. Kind of like what she'd done with the iris. She opened her eyes and nothing had changed. Echo battled with the monsters, leaping and twisting around their legs as they gave chase. But one had figured out the ruse. It swiveled sunken sockets toward Cas.

Cas closed her eyes again and willed the chains into being. She had no idea what she was doing. And somehow, no matter how hard she pushed, something pushed back. That wasn't quite right. Something was holding her back, like a straight-jacket pulled tight.

She strained until her head ached while ignoring the sounds of her friend fighting for their lives. "Oh please, work. Work!" she begged.

Cas sensed the thing that bound her was designed to resist brute force. Instead of pushing, she decided to pull. She envisioned it just like a straight-jacket, pinching, binding, and cinched in place with locks. In her mind's eye, she took one of those and leaned every ounce of her being on it.

The lock buckled. Not much—it only opened a crack. But it was enough. Cas envisioned thick, bulky chains and flung them out at the monsters.

Cas opened her eyes. One of the monsters stood only a foot away. Arm outstretched, its claws were only inches away from her face. But it didn't move. The spell worked! Only the eyes shifted to fix a death-like glare on her.

She sidestepped around that one to look beyond. The other creatures were frozen in place too. Echo swatted at a monster's ankle. "And take that."

A finger on the outstretched hand closest to Cas twitched. She saw it and knew whatever she had done was wearing off already.

"Echo! Come on!" she hollered and made a final dash for the gates. Cas crashed into them and clawed at the padlock and chains. Echo skidded to a stop next to her. But it was no good. There was no give. She pushed at the gates, but the space that opened was too small to squeeze through.

"Whatever you're going to do, do it fast!"

Cas whirled around. What now? She didn't think and just ran along the fence line with Echo.

Without warning, the creatures all seemed to break the spell in unison. They roared. Cas refused to look but sensed movement behind her and to the right.

The things jeered as the gap between them and Cas shortened. Fifteen feet away, they cackled. "Where ya going, sweetheart?"

Then, at ten feet, they sang and cackled, "No place to go."

In her mind, she threw the chains out again. But Cas didn't have to look to know it didn't work. She could feel it. And somehow, the monsters did too. They looked at each other and began to laugh. Suddenly, they all dove at once, blocking out her view of the twilight sky behind them.

Cascade dove toward the metal gate. She shoved, pushed, and forced her body through the bars. Somehow, she found a spot just big enough to squeeze through. Skeletal fingertips grasped at her sneaker just as she fell to the sidewalk. Echo, more nimble, made his escape almost simultaneously. He landed next to Cas.

She collapsed on the ground outside the gate. The skeletal creatures screamed in fury. They clawed at the bars and shrieked in frustration until it seemed they lost interest and drifted away.

Echo rubbed his head against Cas' cheek. "You did it, Cas. You're safe," he purred.

"What were those?" she panted.

Echo flopped on his side. "Ghouls."

Cas nodded. Another supernatural term that had meant nothing a few days ago. "You okay?"

"Nothing a plate of tuna wouldn't fix."

"Echo, I'm you're woman for tuna for the rest of your life." Cas rolled over and focused on breathing in and out. Her heart still beat a wicked staccato. Cas was so relieved to see an unfettered sky, she almost wept.

After collecting herself, Cas got up and sat on the curb outside the cemetery gate. Echo rose up on his haunches, and they were both silent. A bunch of questions about ghouls, bindings, and spells bubbled to her mind, but she didn't have the energy to form the words. Plus, she had the hiccups.

Firecracker sounds erupted just to the left of them. They weren't as powerful as when she had caused the car pile-up but still plenty loud. Cas felt a surge of annoyance. She pushed at the magical restraint. It was still there. And so was the small crack she had created. Without ghouls on the chase, she could sense it now. Cas dropped her head into her hands. This nonsense was just baffling.

Her magic could make all kinds of irritating things happen, but she couldn't even use it to keep ghouls from eating her. If she had to have magical powers, shouldn't she at least be able to use them to avoid being devoured by cemetery dwelling nightmare creatures?

"Don't like ghouls much, eh?"

Afraid the ghouls had gotten out of the cemetery, Cas jumped up from the curb and spun around. But it wasn't a monster just inside the cemetery side of the gate. It looked like a person, but Cas deduced it was a ghost.

It didn't hover like Denzel but stood on two feet like Violaine. Cas now knew that's who must have been following her around lately—Violette's dead twin sister.

This ghost was male, about eighteen years old, and bore a giant smirk on his face. He sported a white t-shirt and a ripped-up pair of jeans. "If you don't like the undead, you shouldn't go visiting certain graves around here at twilight. You're only asking for trouble if you do." He turned and sprinted away, fading into the darkness.

Why would visiting her mom's grave make ghouls attack her?

She heard a faint sound. It grew in intensity until a bright yellow Ford Escape with blue and white flashing lights and a wailing siren screeched to a stop in front of her and Echo. Three men and a woman dressed in coveralls that matched the car jumped out and approached them.

"Peacekeeper squad," Echo said by way of explanation to Cas. She nodded.

A black Ford Escape with *Sheriff* stamped on the side in big, yellow letters pulled up behind the other car. Deputy Chris Wave jumped out of the driver's side. He rolled his eyes at the peacekeepers but joined their ranks as they surrounded Cas and Echo.

"What's going on here? We got an alert that you slipped your leash," the woman said.

"It's about time. Do you know how long ago I broke that thing off?" Cas snapped, peering up at them from the curb. "I was attacked by ghouls—that's what happened! In the cemetery long before it should've closed. I snapped the darn thing off hoping you all would rush to my rescue, but so much for that." Cas threw her hands up in distaste. She didn't feel like being polite or mincing words.

"It says here you're supposed to have bindings on too," one of the men said as he consulted a clipboard. He pulled a set of goggles down from the top of his head over his eyes and peered at Cas through them. "Yep. Still there, but they're snapped in a couple of places. It's not bad enough that we can't fix it, though."

"Gee, thanks," Cas mumbled.

The four peacekeepers held hands and surrounded Cas. They began to rhythmically chant and continued to do so for several minutes. When they stopped and dropped hands, Cas felt the full dampening effect of the bindings return.

The deputy leaned against the fence and popped gum while the witches did their work. "Don't see any ghouls now."

Graham's white Silverado pulled up behind the peacekeeper squad's Ford, and he jumped out. "What happened?" He jogged over to Cas and touched her arm. He looked her over with a critical eye. "Are you hurt?"

"Just a few scrapes, I think." She held up her forearm. The slash wasn't bad. Neither was the one on her upper arm. She'd gotten lucky.

One of the male peacekeepers leaned over. "It's not bad. Ghouls don't have venom. But if the cold doesn't infect you, bacteria might. They're no better than rats. I have some disinfectant wash in the truck. Be right back."

Cas dropped her arm and said, "I'll probably have some bruises tomorrow, but they'll just blend in with the ones I got earlier." She sighed, feeling defeated. Deputy Wave made his way over with another leash in hand. He said nothing, just motioned for Cas to stick her arm out.

"Ghouls chased her out of the cemetery," Echo explained to Graham as Deputy Wave placed the new leash on Cas' wrist. He ignored Graham and touched Cas as little as possible. He activated the leather without comment and then got in his car and drove away.

"The gates closed early," Cas told Graham, whose eyes narrowed at the news.

The peacekeeper washed and dressed Cas' wounds. "We'll take a ride around the cemetery. Make sure nothing got out or in," he finished with a smirk.

They left Cas underwhelmed. "No wonder they haven't found the stone yet."

Graham glanced over into the cemetery, but everything was quiet. "Let's get you home." He led her to the truck. She climbed up into the passenger seat. Cas thanked the heavens for a good ol' fashioned car instead of a courser. Echo jumped up and curled into a ball in the back seat. The truck rumbled to life just before Graham pulled away from the curb.

Cas nestled into the seat and closed her eyes. When she opened them again, Graham was pulling into her driveway.

The three of them entered Cas' house in silence, and she turned the kitchen light on. She put a kettle of water on to heat up and rummaged around in the refrigerator for something to eat. She pulled out some leftover roast chicken along with bread, mayonnaise, and lettuce.

As the three of them sat and drank tea (non-dairy milk for Echo) and ate chicken sandwiches, Cas and Echo told Graham the story of what had happened at the cemetery.

"So you stopped and looked at Violaine Mizzle's headstone right before the ghouls attacked?" Graham verified.

"Yes, I did." Something occurred to Cas and her eyes widened. "Do you think that's the gravesite the ghost meant when he said I shouldn't go visiting certain graves if I don't like the undead?"

Graham shrugged. "Maybe." He took a bite of sandwich and chewed for a few minutes. "Actually, I think that's a pretty good bet, considering it sounds like the ghost from that grave has been following you."

Cas thought for a second. "Makes sense. Well, I don't have anywhere else to go to follow the leads we have on Sapphire, Bear Barns, or Dzovag Livings. So maybe I'll pay a visit to Violette Mizzle tomorrow."

Chapter 14

Cas grabbed a sweater just in case the fall morning weather was cool. Seeing Violette was on the agenda for today. But first, another trip to the Courthouse. If she spent any more time there, Cas might as well rent out space and take up residence. She chuckled. The huge, gothic building sure seemed to be her second home since everything had started. Though this would be a short visit. She just needed to find out a couple of things.

Cas stuck her head into the doorway of the extra bedroom. Echo snoozed away on the bed. "Echo." She waited few seconds and called his name again. "Hey, it's time to head out."

The cat mumbled, rolled over, and scratched his bared belly with a paw. When he started to snore, Cas got the hint. Echo wasn't going anywhere, anytime soon. She glanced at her watch and grimaced. It was still early, but Cas didn't want the morning to slip by. Today was a big day in Crystal Springs and people would be out and about. She didn't want to chance missing Violette.

Echo was supposed to be a safeguard in case anything went wrong with her power. Cas flexed against the magical bindings. They pulsed in response and felt strong. Since the peacekeepers had renewed them, her magic hadn't acted up. Perhaps a quick visit into Crystal Springs without a chaperone wouldn't do any harm. After all, she was an adult.

She left a note on the bed for Echo, though she wasn't quite sure if the cat could read, and tiptoed out of the house. It was warm, and she tossed the sweater into the passenger seat of her car. Cas drove the old, beat-up, silver Dodge Intrepid to the Courthouse—she really needed to learn to call a courser.

Dustin, who was the only one around, didn't hesitate to offer his assistance as usual.

"Yes, Violaine Mizzle is a registered ghost who's allowed to leave the cemetery," he said. They stood in the council chamber, and Dustin looked at the same book he'd used the day before to find out whether Cas' mom was a ghost.

He then grabbed the witch's lineage volume. It took him longer to page through that one, but he finally said, "Ah, here she is. Violette Mizzle. She lives at 17 Hucklebuck Avenue in the Riverside Condos. Nice places." He shut the book and smiled, but his gaze was intense. "Are you getting anywhere with determining who killed the Archsiren?"

"Not really. Mostly, I'm just trying to keep myself busy and out of trouble while I hope some big clue falls in my lap. Thanks for all your help."

"You're welcome. I like you. And I always root for the underdog." Dustin winked. He escorted Cas out of the chamber and back down the hall to the reception area. "Good luck. Will you be attending the Founder's Day parade tonight?"

"Oh, I hadn't thought about it. Maybe."

"Great, I hope to see you there. It's always a blast."

They said good-bye, and Cas headed out to the car. She punched Violette's address into her phone and set it to voice direct.

It felt good to do something normal like drive and to have some independence. It gave Cas some confidence about this new reality she'd found herself in. She began to sing along, off-tune, with the pop song on the radio, turned the volume up, and rolled the window down.

Violette lived on the edge of Crystal Springs. Cas pulled into the driveway after about fifteen minutes of singing and enjoying the feeling of the breeze on her face. She walked up the driveway toward the condo's front door but then paused. Cas rooted around in her purse for some lipstick, using the moment as an opportunity to evaluate her feelings.

Deep down, Cas knew talking to Violette made sense. She suspected the woman could reveal something about what was going on and maybe even explain the role her mother had played in it.

Ah, that was where the reluctance was, she realized. She didn't want to hear if her mom had somehow been involved. So many people had accused Oceane of being a mischief-maker—a girl who got into trouble. Cas wasn't sure she wanted to know those particular details about her mother. She wanted to remember her as a good mom.

Cas swallowed hard, flipped open a handheld mirror, and applied a swipe of lipstick. She smacked her lips together and then took a deep breath. She was an adult, and her mother had been gone for a long time. This needed to be done. How could Cas ever truly understand herself and what was happening if she didn't?

Cas tucked the lipstick away, put her purse on her shoulder, straightened her spine, and marched without any more hesitation up to Violette's front door. She rapped hard four times.

Within seconds, the door opened wide, and Violette stood on the other side. She wore a light blue dress that came down to her knees. The long hair, mostly still auburn like her sister's but streaked with silver, hung in a braid draped over one shoulder.

She smiled, though it didn't reach her eyes. "Come on in, Cascade. I've been expecting your visit."

Cas raised her eyebrows. "You have?"

Violette nodded. "After the cemetery, I figured you might put two and two together and come see me."

Cas didn't know what to say to that. She walked in and waited for Violette to close the door and lead the way to a small living room. It was cozy, all done in cream and three shades of light green. A big fireplace was the focal point of one wall, and opposite that was a large window that overlooked a private courtyard.

Violette directed Cas to a mint green rocking chair with a matching footstool. She asked if she could get her anything. Cas shook her head, and Violette sat on the sofa across from Cas. "What do you need to know?" Violette asked, her voice steady but just above a whisper.

Cas started to speak but no words came out. She cleared her throat and uncrossed and re-crossed her ankles before trying again. This time, her voice was strong and clear. "You're my mom's age, I think. You knew her, didn't you?"

"Yes. I knew Oceane." There was no hesitation. Violette had expected that question too.

"How?"

"She, Lavania, and I had a clique."

Cas leaned forward a little. Violette was forthcoming but also seemed sad. Almost like she'd been waiting for the day the truth could come out. "You mean you were friends in school or something?"

The corners of Violette's mouth twitched. "Well, we did know each other from school but, no, dear. A clique in this instance is a supernatural thing. It's when a number of witches come together temporarily to perform some complicated or dangerous magic that requires more than one person. It's usually something that's beneficial to all members of the clique."

"What magic were you three doing together?" Her boldness had retreated a little, and Cas almost couldn't get the words out. A lump had formed in her throat. She knew there was no going back after this question was asked and answered. Whatever Violette told her now about her mom, Cas would never be able to un-know it.

"Lavania had a perpetuity stone. She'd somehow stolen it from the Archsiren at the time, Ranger Helm. We didn't ask too many questions about that. Anyway, she had a stone and we all wanted to do something with it."

Cas wished she had asked for a drink. It would be nice to have something to fidget with. She settled for rubbing the handle of her purse between a thumb and forefinger. "What things does a perpetuity stone do?"

Violette tipped her head to the side and looked past Cas at the wall behind her. When she answered, Cas got the sense she was revisiting thoughts and feelings from decades ago. "It's a really rare magical artifact that captures the energy essence of a powerful witch. Then, if you're pretty powerful yourself—or you have a clique—you can channel some of that energy and cast big spells. We wanted to make webs."

Cas' stomach plunged. But there was no turning back now. "What are webs?"

Violette sat back on the sofa and took a deep breath. Then she scooted forward again. "Are you sure you wouldn't like anything to drink?" Her gaze focused back on Cas, returned to the current time and place.

The sharp change of topic caught Cas off-guard, but she decided to take advantage of a break in the conversation. "Some water would be great."

Violette rose. She seemed to flow across the floor, and Cas thought the woman must have a dance background. Cas followed her into the kitchen. It was a cheerful, bright room with white cupboards and appliances. Frilly white valances decorated with strawberries hung at the windows, and other red accents, like a toaster and some red-framed photos, dotted the space.

Violette got a glass from the cupboard, filled it with ice from the dispenser on the outside of the refrigerator, and then added water. She didn't get any for herself.

Violette handed the glass to Cas. "A web is a spell that sets off a complicated series of events to reach a desired endpoint. It's a difficult spell to cast and usually requires a clique and a ton of magical oomph. With the stone, our threesome had both, so we figured we could all get what we desired. Lavania craved power. She wanted to use the stone to become the Archsiren.

Your mother had just given birth to you. She was more than a little scared about how she'd be able to provide. Oceane thought finding a rich man would give you—and herself—everything you both might ever want. And I . . ." Violette hesitated and then sighed. "My sister wasn't born with magic. More than anything else, I—we—wanted her to have powers like I did."

Cas took a drink of water. She thought about the three women who each wanted something so specific and big to happen in their lives. It reminded her of stories she'd read when she was younger about people who made deals with the devil. "So the three of you did these web spells together with the perpetuity stone. Did they work?"

"Oh yes. They worked. If you have the power to cast them, webs always work." Violette said. Her voice quavered a tiny bit. "But not usually in the way you expect. Predicting all the outcomes of a web is sort of like dropping a pebble in a pond and trying to guess where the ripples will go. When you cast one, you must be sure you're willing to accept the consequences. We thought we were, but it's really not possible to foresee the impact."

She paused and moved around the end of the counter to stand closer to Cas. "Lavania became the Archsiren, but the cost was the death of the previous one, Ranger. My sister got her power, but not the time and experience to control it. It was too much too fast. Violaine attempted magic beyond her skill and was killed as a result."

Cas sat silent for a moment, horrified at the thought of two deaths from the webs the three women cast. She didn't want to ask the next question, but it was ultimately the one she needed the answer to the most. "And my mom's web?"

"It worked, of course. Your mother found a man of means to care for the two of you. But it ultimately resulted in her death too. At least, that's what I believe. I can't really prove it. It just took longer for the strings of magic to accomplish that tragic end for her. And now, Lavania's paid the same price." Violette looked down. "I fear the web will catch me eventually as well."

Cas felt as if a shard of ice impaled her chest. Her mother's death might have been triggered by Oceane's own hand. All in an attempt to meet Cas' stepfather. It seemed superficial, stupid, and selfish. Since her step-father had sent her away after her mother's death, Cas ended up unhappy despite being well provided for financially.

She wanted to ask how Violette thought the web and her mom's death were related. Cas had always believed her mom died of cancer. But then another question pushed forward and demanded attention. "You said the perpetuity stone harnessed the energy of a powerful witch that you then used to cast your web spells."

Violette nodded to encourage Cas to ask the question.

"Whose power did you capture in the stone?"

Violette only hesitated for a fraction of a second. "Yours."

Cas had foreseen the answer, but it still made her swallow hard. She set the water glass on the kitchen counter. Her fingers trembled.

Violette grabbed her hand and squeezed. She guided Cas to a seat at the kitchen table and sat close. "Most witches blossom at puberty. But once in a while, a special witch is born. One who has power from birth and who is given the label of supreme. You had that type of power. In fact, the power you had—have—is extremely rare." Violette looked off into the distance for a minute. "Tempeste has such power, and she's in town this week. The last time a witch of equal power visited Crystal Springs, to my knowledge, was the year you were born."

She turned back to Cas. "We siphoned your power into the perpetuity stone that Lavania brought us. We wanted to cast our webs, yes, but we rationalized that we were helping you too. As a baby with such immense power, we told ourselves that you could easily hurt yourself or others. We decided we'd store your powers until you were of an age when most witches blossom naturally. In the meantime, we'd cast our webs and make life better for all of us."

Violette stopped and waited for Cas' reaction, but Cas didn't know what to say. She pulled her hand away from Violette. There was so much to digest. Her mind felt thick and heavy. She was a super powerful witch, but her birth-right had been taken…stolen actually, and used in a manner that had hurt people.

Her *mother* had set this in motion.

A sudden sharp pain brought Cas back to the moment. She looked down at her hand. Her palm was embedded with half-moons. She'd been digging her nails into the skin and hadn't realized. This was beyond what Cas could've guessed. It was going to take some time to process.

As Violette watched Cas' face, she seemed to understand and gave a little nod. "Lavania and Oceane didn't want to give up the stone, even after they saw the horrible effects their spells had. So I stole it. I took it to SunSprite and gave them instructions to deliver the package on your sixteenth birthday. I felt it was the only way to keep the others from being tempted to use the stone more and to protect you. If anyone got their hands on the stone, you'd be in danger. My sister agreed."

Violette shook her head. She stood and began to pace around the small room, agitated. "As you've probably noticed, we were able to get Violaine registered and licensed to leave the cemetery. Even I didn't know how often she's been checking up on you throughout the years. When you turned sixteen and didn't get your package, we were both horrified. SunSprite has given us the runaround ever since. Those sprites are harder to nail down than a slippery serpent at Halloween time." Her voice had a hard edge that had been absent before. "Somehow, they miraculously found the package a few days ago—more than thirty years late."

Violette stopped her pacing and went back to Cas. She bent over, grabbed both of Cas' hands, and looked intently into her eyes. "I'm so sorry your life was so disrupted by our selfishness. We rationalized what we did as being good for you too, but it wasn't. Now you're fifty years old and trying to learn to deal with your immense powers. Forgive us. Forgive me.

"But maybe I can be of help. I could mentor you, at least a little bit. I'm nowhere near your power level, but maybe I could start to teach you the basics anyway. If the council approves."

Cas wrapped her arms around herself. She couldn't look the other woman in the eye. "Thank you for the offer. I'll ask the council about it. And thank you for your honesty. I have to go now."

She headed for the door with Violette close behind. Cas put a hand on the doorknob but turned around. "I don't know how to feel right now. The three of you changed my life in ways I can't even imagine." Cas paused to take a deep breath. "But thank you for trying to get the stone to me. You and Violaine."

Cas looked up at Violette. The other woman's eyes brimmed with unshed tears. She stood a little taller, as if a weight had been removed from her shoulders. Cas said, "I have to get going, but perhaps I'll visit you when I'm up for it. I'd love to hear more about my mom."

"Of course. Come anytime you're ready," Violette answered.

Cas stepped outside and paused. "By the way, where is Violaine?" She looked over Violette's shoulder back into the house.

"Oh, she comes and goes. But ever since you've regained your abilities, I've been seeing her less. I think Violaine is more at peace now. I could summon her if you'd like to talk."

"No, that's okay." Cas couldn't say *no thanks* fast enough. She didn't know what summoning a ghost involved, but Cas didn't have the mental capacity to handle much more. "Bye, Violette."

She got in her car and sat there for a minute, fiddling with the keys. Some of it was just too much to parse at the moment. Over the years, the details of Oceane's face had faded in Cas' mind. But right now, her mom's image was clear and sharp. So sharp it stung. Cas wiped at her eyes.

Instead of thinking of her mother, she ran through the entire conversation with Violette and tried to look at it through a critical lens of what was happening now—her being framed for Lavania's murder.

Cas backed out of the driveway. She didn't have a destination in mind—her thoughts swirled around like clouds, wispy and just out of grasp. As she drove, she worked to pin down one of them to be examined.

A WITCH TOO LATE

Lavania didn't have an absence of enemies. First, there were her fellow sirens. Cas had seen firsthand how the Archsiren had no problem showering insults on them. Years of abuse could push anyone over the edge. And each of the other council members had the power to murder Lavania in the way she'd been killed.

And what about the other citizens of Crystal Springs? There was that Dzovag man. He'd been raging all over town about how Lavania had blocked his lavish hotel plans. And Cas couldn't forget that Bear guy at the newspaper. Though his wife seemed capable of calming him down.

Sapphire, her half-sister's assistant, had a bone to pick with Lavania too. But as Cas thought of the diminutive woman, it was hard to picture her having the magical oomph to accomplish murder. But what if she'd gotten her hands on some type of taboo thingamajig off the black market? Hadn't the illegal dealing leprechaun, Seamus, been at the same convention? Could they have done a deal?

Cas let loose an impatient huff. All this work and she was no closer to discovering the identity of Lavania's killer. Maybe she should get each of the sirens alone and somehow encourage them to talk.

Suddenly, something Violette said leaped into the forefront of her mind. Lavania had stolen the perpetuity stone, a very rare magical item, from Ranger, the previous Archsiren. A question stirred in Cas' brain: Why did Ranger have the artifact in the first place?

When Cas' dousing amulet was destroyed, the sirens had ordered Dustin to dispose of it discretely because Shiloh had bought it off the magical black market. Didn't the council say any items that tampered with a witch's power were illegal? If so, why would an Archsiren need a perpetuity stone?

If Ranger had somehow acquired one, he must have planned to use it for something.

And what if the reappearance of the stone now was somehow connected to Lavania's death?

Cas' attention snapped back to the present. She'd driven to the hot springs on auto-pilot. This wasn't her first visit. Like many residents living close to Crystal Springs, Cas enjoyed the touristy spots too.

She parked, got out of the car, and stretched her back. There were only two other cars in the parking lot. She grinned, amused at herself. Her subconscious mind must have known this would be a good spot to think.

The springs were at the end of a short path that led through a copse of trees just off the parking lot. Cas took her time making her way down it, breathing in the forest scents and drinking in the nature sights. There had been a brief rain early that morning, and drops of water on the leaves and grass caused the colors to pop even more vividly.

As the woods ended, Cas heard the sound of the river. The path opened up to reveal a large clearing filled with huge rocks surrounding a steaming pool of water. Cas shed her shoes and socks and climbed up to perch on a boulder. She could feel warm air billowing at her face from the hot spring and something else pulsing in the air too. It felt similar to the calm, compelling feeling Cas experienced when Tempeste had been nearby in the council chamber. This must be the power she'd heard was associated with the hot springs. She'd never noticed it before.

As Tempeste crossed her mind, another thought hit her, and she gasped and sat up straighter, fully alert. Violette said that a witch of Tempeste's power had visited Crystal Springs the year Cas was born. The year her mother and the others stole the perpetuity stone from Ranger. Had he planned to capture that visiting witch's power in the stone and use it for something?

Pieces of the puzzle clicked together more rapidly now. She could feel that she was close to the answer. Still, one big question remained, the answer to which might lead to Lavania's killer.

What type of spell had Archsiren Ranger wanted to cast with the magic harnessed from a powerful witch?

She thought about the reasons Violette, Lavania, and Oceane wanted to cast webs. Could one of those be the same reason Ranger wanted to use the stone? He was already Archsiren, so it couldn't be that. Did he want more power? More money? Maybe. She didn't understand all the benefits that came with the position.

As she questioned those two motives, Violette's reason for casting a web floated into Cas' mind and captured her attention: *To help a family member.*

Had Ranger been desperate to help someone?

Possibly. Actually, it seemed probable.

But who had Ranger wanted to help? Cas thought it had to be someone in the man's family. It seemed unlikely that he would risk a web spell's backlash and negative consequences for a mere friend or acquaintance.

Could any of that be connected to Lavania's death? Cas didn't know anything about Archsiren Ranger's family, but she knew where to go to find out. She grabbed her shoes and headed back toward the parking lot. She moved much faster than earlier. She didn't pause to take in the sights or sounds this time.

When she got back to the edge of the lot, more vehicles had pulled in. Dzovag Livings was there. "This patch of trees will need to be taken down and the parking lot expanded to cover that area," he said to another man, who nodded and scribbled on a yellow legal pad. "The main hotel building will go over there." Dzovag pointed toward the river.

The other man nodded again and then looked up from his pad. "And you have all the necessary permits for this, sir?"

Dzovag's face turned red. "I will," he sputtered. "I have no doubt of that now. My obstacle has been removed."

Maybe it was the exasperation about her mom. Perhaps it was her mounting frustration about solving Lavania's murder. But whatever the trigger, Cas couldn't resist stepping up to them. "What do you mean by that?"

Dzovag's eyes were the first to respond. They snapped in Cas' direction before his bulk followed. "I've heard of you. You're that...well rumor says no one can figure out what you are. A freak of nature perhaps. But I guess I owe you a debt of gratitude."

Cas stood her ground. "I haven't done anything to be thanked for."

"Nonsense. Lavania's death has done this town a service."

"I didn't kill her. What about you? Is that what you meant by an obstacle being removed? Lavania? Did you remove her?"

Dzovag chuckled and flicked an invisible speck off his tie. "I'm more of a lover and business man than fighter."

Cas stepped back and made a show of looking the man over from head to toe. She titled her head to one side. "I doubt that. The lover part, I mean."

The man with the pad stifled a laugh. Dzovag's eyes swiveled to him and back to Cas. He took a step forward, close enough to invade Cas' personal space. "You need be careful. I'm not a man to be treated carelessly."

"And if the rumors you heard are true, you should know threatening me is a bad idea. I might lose control." Cas waggled her fingers in his face.

Dzovag jerked away and blustered. "Go away. We have business."

"My pleasure. I have to get to the Courthouse anyway."

Cas pivoted, feeling surprised by her outburst. Yet, it had felt satisfying too. Speaking her mind had been long overdue. Though maybe telling a potential killer her next location hadn't been a good idea. Oh well. It was too late to worry about that. She hopped into her car, started it, and left the parking lot.

Cas glanced at the clock on the dashboard and was shocked to see that it was 6:00 pm. The day had flown by, and she hadn't eaten anything other than a banana before she left the house. Her stomach growled.

Her cell rang. It was Graham. Echo had come to his place looking for her. Cas filled him in and agreed to meet them outside the Courthouse to watch the Founder's Day parade, but after they hung up, all she could think about was Ranger and what he might have been up to with the perpetuity stone.

She had to park a few streets away from the Courthouse because traffic was barred from entering the mile-long area around what would be the parade route, including the street right in front of the building. A crowd had already gathered and started celebrating, and more people poured into the area every minute. Cas had to squeeze her way between revelers to make any headway in getting to the front door of the Courthouse.

She tried not to bump into anyone, but it was impossible. She brushed against a passerby. "Oh, I'm sorry," she murmured.

The woman snorted in response and Cas looked at her face for the first time. She had jet black hair, cats-eye makeup, and three tiny horns protruding from her forehead. She scrunched up her nose and hissed at Cas. Her tongue was the same shade of black as her hair and had a fork like a snake's.

Cas raised her eyebrows and moved her head back as much as she could. Then she smiled. "I love your makeup. I wish that style looked good on me," she said. The other woman's lower jaw dropped down about an inch and Cas held her breath.

Then the fork-tongued woman smiled back. It transformed her whole face. "I watch makeup tutorials on the internet for a couple hours every evening to unwind," she said. "It helps with the anger issues that come along with being a lesser demon. Serpentine blood tends to run hot, ya know? But tonight I can leave my horns out and not disguise my tongue. Happy Founder's Day!"

Cas nodded and continued to press through the crowd, proud of herself for making a connection. Maybe she could get used to moving through the supernatural community after all.

She made it to the Courthouse and tried the doors. Locked, of course. It was after hours and most people would be at the parade. But she was on to something, Cas could feel it.

She moved back to let some parade-goers pass by and then fell in step behind them.

At the corner of the Courthouse, she ducked out of the flow of foot-traffic. If the front doors were locked, why would the back be open? But there were residences somewhere in the huge building, so there must be a way in. Unless the people who lived here used some magical means to zap in or whatever. Well, trying wouldn't hurt.

It took her almost a full trip around the building, but Cas did find another entrance. A big 'ol lobby with blazing lights and a sign that said *Residences* above it. It was just around the other side from the Courthouse entrance she usually used. She felt silly for never noticing it before.

At least the lobby didn't have a doorman. Cas walked in without being questioned. And right where she would've guessed it would be was an unmarked metal door. The knob turned without much effort. Cas peeked in and—jackpot—there was the cavernous vestibule of the Courthouse.

The place looked deserted. She didn't see anyone milling about on the main floor. Maybe this would be easy.

She took the hover pad up to the level that housed the council chamber and moved down the hallway to the reception area. The door was unlocked, but neither Waverly nor Denzel manned the tall desk.

The air was silent and still, as if there wasn't a soul in the entire building. But she was technically breaking and entering. Was this really a good idea? Cas made her decision a split second later. She didn't want to wait another day to get answers.

Cas darted behind the reception desk and tested the door. It yielded under her hand, and she stuck her head into the hallway beyond. It was empty and quiet. *Awesome.*

She crept down the hallway to the closed door leading to the council chamber. Cas glanced around one last time but still didn't see or hear anyone. The biggest threat to being caught was Denzel. The ghost might be able to hear better than any humans in the vicinity. But then again, ghosts could like parades too, right? After all, lesser demons, sprites, and sirens did. She held her breath and twisted the chamber door's knob.

It didn't open. She'd been afraid of that.

Cas examined the lock. It was a simple, turning knob with a keyhole. Piece of cake. One credit card from her purse and a minute or two of stealthy finesse, and the latch opened with a soft pop.

"Yes!" she whispered. All those times getting locked out the house and jimmying the back door had paid off.

She slipped into the council chamber and closed the door. Cas crossed to the smooth wall where Dustin had pulled the witch lineage book from. The wall was smooth.

Crap. She'd forgotten about this part. Okay, okay. She could do this.

Cas took a deep breath, closed her eyes, and thought back to what Dustin had done after the Table of Contents had flapped into the wall. She studied the entire scene in her mind's eye. Just do what he did.

The wall was totally blank and flat. Cas prayed this was a parlor trick anyone could do and not something that required powers. What if there was some type of magical protection or lock? Losing a finger was not on today's agenda.

Well, no pain, no gain or something like that. Cas gritted her teeth and swatted at the wall like it was a pesky gnat. It sucked her hand in up to the wrist, and she forced herself not to jump back.

She couldn't see her hand. But it tingled as if it had plunged into liquid twenty degrees colder than the rest of the room. Her fingers grazed something hard, and Cas gave it a hard yank.

A book! She looked at the cover. It read, *Magical Princes of Medieval Spain*. Wrong one. She frowned, disappointed. But giving up wasn't an option now. Not when she was this close.

She set the book down on a shelf that had appeared when she'd pulled the book out. Cas moved half a step to her right and repeated the wall-grabbing motion. This time, when she withdrew her hand, it held a book she recognized. It was huge, and she needed two hands to balance the thing.

Cas set it down and flipped open the cover, hoping for some kind of index to find the family history of Archsiren Ranger.

Pain exploded in the back of her head, and before everything went dark, she thought, *Wow, Denzel really hits hard for a ghost.*

Chapter 15

Cas' head felt like fire. No, not fire. Lava. It felt as if molten rock had been poured into her skull. With every second that consciousness returned, the burning pain ratcheted up a notch.

She moaned and touched the base of her skull. That was a mistake. Another white-hot throb pulled a groan from her lips. Her fingers came away flecked with the warm, sticky residue of half-dried blood. For a second, she wished to pass out again but then it struck her.

Someone had hit her.

A cold chill traveled down her body from head to toes. This was bad. She needed to get up now. Cas glanced down. That was going to a problem. Whoever had knocked her out had also trussed her up like a pig. A strong, shiny material bound her wrists. A short length of it extended to her feet and snaked around them.

She was tied up on the floor of the council chamber. She should've noticed that already. Her thoughts felt sluggish, as if they had to travel through layers of cotton. Cas blinked hard, hoping that would clear her head, and then she groaned again. The small movement triggered another wave of agony. She took three longs breaths to center herself.

Who had hit her?

Denzel? She'd been worried about him walking in at the wrong time. Cas opened her eyes. She couldn't see anyone. She held her breath and listened.

Far away, a dull roar went off. The parade had started. Cas strained to pick up any noise—the shuffling of feet or someone else breathing. Nothing.

But another sense whispered something different.

Her heart fluttered like a terrified bird's. Whoever had tied her up had their reasons. They weren't going to just let her go.

"Hello?" she called out to the dim room.

No, that was stupid, Cas chided herself. She tested her bonds. They held fast.

Dzovag Livings. *Livings.*

This was what she got for her temper tantrum at the spring. Livings or a hired thug had come for payback.

It made sense. He had every motive to kill Lavania. He, for sure, would not have appreciated Cas snooping around.

But she wasn't going to wait to find out for sure. Cas struggled against her bindings, but every way she twisted only made the knots tighter. She needed something sharp to cut the material.

Right, like the attacker would've left a handy-dandy pair of scissors within reach. But maybe she could manifest a pair?

Cas attempted to pull an image into her mind. But the magical bindings didn't like it. They didn't pulse in response like before. This time, something invisible slapped her face. Hard. It sent her head throbbing.

This was the first time Cas had attempted magic on purpose since Tempeste had bound her. The binding spell resisted—big time. *Wonderful.*

She struggled to get into a sitting position. The wall that held the lineage book was close. She scooted toward it slowly. Once there, maybe she could use it as leverage to get on her feet.

Behind her, someone laughed. "Tempeste did a good job, huh?" The voice, low and deep, came from across the room. "Where are my manners? Here, let me help you." Heavy foot-falls echoed against the chamber's walls. As the person got closer, the pace slowed.

The footsteps stopped just behind Cas. Whoever it was towered over her, taking long, shuddering breaths. Cas refused to turn around, knowing that if she did, it would be the moment the first blow would fall.

Instead, she pushed ever so gently against the magical locks that cinched her powers down tight.

After a while, the person seemed to get bored waiting and, with an exasperated snort, took another step.

Cas couldn't help it now. She looked up.

It was Dustin.

For the briefest of moments, Cas felt a wave a relief. But then Dustin grabbed her upper arms, digging his nails into her skin. He hauled Cas upright and slammed her against the wall in one smooth motion.

The impact was hard enough to send the huge lineage tome tumbling to their feet. Cas' head knocked against the wall with a thud. Everything winked out for a second and then crashed back into focus.

Dustin, the nicest man she'd met in Crystal Springs, had transformed. He leered at her, his face distorting into a grotesque mask. His lips pulled back in a sneer. Before, Dustin had always been the picture of tailored readiness, but now his hair was disheveled and clothes wrinkled.

And was that a speck of red on his face? Cas recoiled. Was that her blood?

Dustin had knocked her out?

He noticed her studying his face and sneered. "What are you looking at?" He wiped at his face with the back of a hand. But the motion only served to turn the small crimson dot into a smear.

Dustin let go of her arms and stepped back. He dusted off his hands as if they'd been handling something vile. Cas was grateful for the space. The anger radiating off him was palpable. She could almost taste it. Dustin stumbled over the lineage book but managed to right himself. He glanced down, screamed a few obscenities, and kicked at the thing. "Curse all of them!"

The gesture struck Cas. Puzzle pieces in her mind starting to turn and shift into place.

It was hard to stand upright with her hands and legs still bound together. She was stuck in a partial hunched-over stance. Cas leaned against the wall and did her best to straighten. "I found out about my mother, Dustin. Did you hear? She hexed me at birth. My own *mother*. So I understand what it's like to have a parent who doesn't do right by their kid."

Cas waited for the words to land. Dustin stared back, open-mouthed. Then he burst into a guffaw of deep-throated laughter.

"Wait, are you saying you're anything like me?" Red blotches crawled up Dustin's neck until they stained his cheeks. "Are you?" Dustin bellowed. But he didn't give her time to answer. He grabbed her face in one hand. "If I was born with your magic, your power, I would be more than a lackey for a group of self-serving prigs. We are nothing alike." Dustin snatched his hand away. "Nothing."

"OK, we're nothing alike. What's going on?" In part, Cas was stalling—for what she didn't know. But on the other hand, he'd been kind to her, and she had liked him. Maybe that part of him could be reasoned with.

"What's going on, dear lady, is that I'm finally going to be Archsiren, as is my birthright."

"Because you're Archsiren Ranger's son, right?" Cas said in the most calming, soothing voice she could muster.

Dustin's eyebrows knit together before he straightened. He kicked at the lineage book again with a yell. "How did you figure it out? I'm only listed under my mother."

Cas spoke as if trying to soothe a fussy child. "I had only a chance to glance at Archsiren Ranger's lineage before, uh, you know..." Dustin stiffened, and Cas changed tack. "I only had a minute to look at his family line. Ranger had a wife, but no children listed."

Dustin turned away. "I was his only son, though not from his marriage. My mother kept the rumors at bay by saying her child's father was a shifter. Witches, snobs that they are, don't bother with listing non-witch parents in their *book*!" He kicked at the tome again, sending it halfway across the room.

Cas wanted to keep him talking. "So your father didn't claim you. What my mother did was worse."

"My father wanted to claim me. He did. When it became clear his marriage wouldn't bear him an heir, he came back to us. But by then, it was obvious..." Dustin voice trailed off, and he stared into space.

Cas used the moment to test both sets of her bindings. The magical ones throbbed in warning. The physical ones tightened.

"Oh, don't bother trying to undo those. The knots are bespelled. You won't be able to slip out short of cutting off a limb."

Cas grimaced. "Could you at least cut the line between my hands and feet so I can stand up straight? This is killing my back."

"Then you should sit," Dustin snapped. He walked over and swept Cas' feet out from underneath her. She fell to the floor with a whoomph.

"That better, dearie?"

"Yeah, thanks." Her backside smarted now. Dustin kept looking at his watch. She wasn't sure what that meant other than time was running out. "So why did your dad get a perpetuity stone?"

"Oh, you figured out that much, huh?"

Cas said nothing but met his stare.

Dustin rolled his eyes. "You are a nosy wench. I knew that woe-is-me act you did in front of the council was a con job. I should've let Lavania kill you, but it's lucky I didn't. You're of so much more use now."

He laid a glare down on Cas that launched a shiver down her neck.

"Dustin," she started, "if you want to do whatever your father was planning, maybe there's another way. People keep telling me how powerful I am. Maybe I can help with whatever you want to do."

He scoffed and squatted in front of Cas. They were eye to eye. "Can you give me magic?"

She cringed, not only from the oddness of the question, but also from his closeness. "What?"

"Magic, Cascade. I was born without magic. Can you grant me that? Can you grant me peace from a lifetime of feeling inadequate in a society of people with wondrous abilities? Can you spare me a life of hiding in plain sight and praying not to be found out?"

"Dustin, I . . ." Cas started, but Dustin waved a dismissive hand and stood.

"You have magic. I've seen you do it," Cas argued.

"Think about it. Have you? When people just assume, it's easy to fool them." His jaw clenched hard, and his eyes narrowed to slits. "I was born without magic—the ultimate insult to a man like my father."

Forget the plan to keep him talking, a part of Cas begged. Right now, she wanted him to shut his trap. Dustin was admitting to things he would never allow to leave this room. He didn't intend to let her out of here alive.

Dustin chuckled, and his facial features evened out. For the moment, he looked more like the man who'd seemed to help her over the past few days. "I'll answer for you. No. It's all Illusions, tricks, and pixie-charms crafted over decades living with the magic-born. When Mother figured out I would never blossom, she helped me hide my disability. We were so good at it, even Father was fooled for a short time."

A WITCH TOO LATE

Dustin knelt down again so his face was on the same level as Cas'. "Father figured it out, though, when I was about fifteen. He was one of the most powerful witches in Crystal Springs, after all." Dustin paused, and a faraway look came over his face. "I'll never forget how he looked when he realized the truth. He was disappointed." He said the last part so softly Cas almost didn't catch it.

If she hadn't been tied up, with a growing knot on the back of her head the size of Wisconsin, Cas might've felt sorry for the man. To be a disappointment to one's parents had to be a horrible burden. The feeling was short-lived, though, as the satiny material cut into her wrists. Everyone has their lot in life. Dustin and his father had no right to hurt others to change theirs.

"Father wasn't the type to be deterred. He was going to have an heir—and a magical one—come dragon's fire or high water."

Cas nodded, which caused searing pain to shoot through her head. She pressed her eyes shut and fought it back down to a burning pain. She said, "Somehow he got his hands on the stone and wanted to use it to cast a web to give you magic."

Dustin chuckled and stood back up. "Not just magic but extraordinary power. He wanted to make up for the mess that fate decreed by neglecting my magical inheritance. He had plans that stretched far beyond Crystal Springs." Dustin paused, and darkness seemed to cover his features again. "But someone meddled and stole the stone from Father before he could use it. And, soon after, he died under strange circumstances. I never knew who had taken the stone. Until this week."

"Lavania," Cas breathed.

The corner of Dustin's mouth rose in a smirk and he spat out, "Lavania. When you came to Court and told the sirens about getting a stone in the mail before your powers blossomed, I knew it had to be a perpetuity stone. I still had no idea how I could get it, but then the Archsiren solved my problem for me. She asked me to help her find your lost stone before the peacekeeper squad could. I asked her why, and she let it slip that she'd used one before and would like to again." Dustin looked down at his hands.

"She used it the year I was born," Cas confirmed.

Dustin's head snapped up. "I didn't intend to kill her, truly." His tone seemed to plead with Cas to believe him, and she nodded and tried to look sympathetic. "I felt such rage when I realized she stole the stone from Father and ruined his plans. Probably even killed him. I murdered her, but I didn't mean to. Once she was dead, I had to think fast. And who else to blame besides a new witch who can't control her powers and whom Lavania had threatened to kill?"

Something white hot and burning burst behind Cas' eyes. It wasn't pain. For the moment, that was gone. This was rage, pure and seething. How dare he frame her for murder? She bit her lip and tempered the rage until it wasn't a wild thing threatening to burst to life. No time for that right now. She had to keep her thoughts as clear as possible and figure out how to stay alive.

"Of course, I kept my ties to the more nefarious aspects of this community throughout the years, always hoping for another perpetuity stone to show up. So when I heard talk of one being around here, I wasted no time finding it. Procuring it from the incubus was nothing."

Cas nodded a little, but her mind had finally cleared. Whenever Dustin took his eyes off her, she scanned the chamber. There had to be something here that could be of help. She said, "You're the one who stole the stone from Mr. Percy."

Dustin inclined his head. He looked proud of himself. "Yes. And I put two and two together. Percy is your neighbor, and he ended up with a perpetuity stone soon after you reported receiving one in the mail. I knew it must be the same stone my father had years ago. What I didn't understand was who sent it to you. I knew it couldn't be Lavania—she'd been desperate to get the stone back."

"Yeah, I don't think Lavania would have let the stone out of her hands on purpose," Cas agreed. She tried to infuse her voice with a mutual distaste for the former Archsiren.

"You probably didn't know that I used to work for SunSprite Deliveries," Dustin volunteered.

Cas shook her head because Dustin seemed to expect an answer.

"It was a part-time job when I was a teenager. I was there for about a year. Long enough to learn my way around the place and discover that curdled milk makes sprites less likely to notice when someone's breaking into their computer system." Dustin sneered again.

Cas remembered how the sprites were drunk on milk when she'd gone to SunSprite to find out who'd sent her the stone. She must have only been a few hours behind Dustin, at the most.

"It was easy for me to find out who sent that package to you," Dustin boasted.

"Violette Mizzle," Cas confirmed.

"Violette," Dustin echoed. "I wagered either she'd stolen the stone from Lavania or had been in on the old crone's plan from the start. I saw her quite often when I went to the cemetery to visit Father." Dustin paused and tilted his head. "I knew she visited Violaine's gravesite often and decided it was time for her to join her sister. I arranged for the cemetery gates to close early and for the ghouls to attack. You being there was just a twist of bad luck."

Dustin reached into his jacket's inside pocket and pulled out the perpetuity stone. It looked the same as when Cas had first seen it.

"Your power is a curse to you," Dustin reasoned. "You're fifty, which is way too old to learn new tricks. Literally. You know nothing of magic. I've been around it my entire life. I'll relieve you of the burden, and you can go back to your normal life. We're just waiting for my companions to join us. Your snooping forced us to act early, but they'll be here soon. I guess I should prepare. Sit tight." He chuckled and walked past her.

Cas understood Dustin wouldn't allow her to leave this room, knowing what she now knew about his crimes. She nodded agreement to encourage him, but he only stoked her rage.

She needed time. If she had any hope of getting out of this room alive, she would need to use her magic. Up until this very second, magic had been a nuisance.

Magic had upheaved her life.

Magic had triggered rejection after rejection.

A WITCH TOO LATE 215

Magic had put her life in jeopardy more than once. Nothing would ever be the same because of it.

But, right now, magic meant life.

She thought hard as Dustin's footsteps faded. He wasn't going to be gone for long. She tried to remember what she'd done to break the bindings when the ghouls attacked her.

The straitjacket! Cas concentrated hard on an image of a straitjacket surrounding her, cinched down with three buckles. The vision sprang to mind easily because she'd done it before.

She mentally leaned into the first buckle with all her might. Cas gave a mental burst and—whap! A backlash made her teeth quiver. It was like a punch to the jaw. No warning pulse this time. The spell that contained her power had retaliated harsh and fast.

She moaned out loud. The sound brought Dustin back into the room. "What are you doing?"

"Nothing. My head just really hurts from where you hit me."

Dustin rounded on her and narrowed his eyes. "No, you're trying to break the bindings Tempeste put on you. It won't work. But just to make my point—"

Cas saw the motion but didn't anticipate it in time to react. Dustin's backhand connected with her temple. The pain was splintering, almost shattering. But something within her flared. It was searing and quick, and the magical constraints billowed the slightest bit. It was just enough to allow her to do one thing.

Hiccup.

A torrent of black confetti burst into the air. It poured into Dustin's mouth and clogged his ears like a swarm of locusts. He screeched and batted at the air while choking and spewing out bits of paper.

The small flair of magic renewed the pain in Cas' head, and she gasped. She worked through the pain. Cas focused on an image in her mind and threw it toward Dustin. Four explosions popped like gunfire—pow, pow, pow, pow—past Dustin's ear, and he scrambled backward fast.

The magical bindings had billowed the slightest bit. But now she could feel the gap she'd forced open closing.

What now? What now? Cas fell onto her side and pushed against the floor to scoot away. It was a futile gesture. A moment later, a hand latched onto her foot and yanked Cas back.

"Cute... and impressive. You've learned some tricks. Maybe you're more like me than I realized." But Dustin flinched when he saw her cold, hard stare. He let out a nervous laugh and squared his shoulders. "I'm not afraid of you." But his body language told another story. He leaned ever-so-slightly away from Cas.

Cas didn't care what he thought. She only cared about making it out of this room and telling everyone about what he had done. Her breath came in heaving gasps as she struggled to push the pain down to a manageable level. Then she lifted her head and stared straight at Dustin.

Undeterred, the fake witch grabbed her arm and tried to haul her upright. But the way she was trussed wouldn't allow Cas to stand. She fell over onto her side, and Dustin swore. "Enough of this."

He pulled a knife from the inside of his jacket. It was a double-edged blade about half a foot long with a brass cross piece.

Cas gasped and shrank away.

"Tsk. It's an athame for ceremonies, dearie. Relax. I can't have you squirming about like a fish." He called for a chair, and just like the first time Cas had visited chambers, one materialized out of the wall and slid to the center of the room.

Dustin severed the length of rope that connected her feet and hands. The other knots didn't loosen. He pulled Cas to her feet with a grunt.

At least she could stand upright now. Dustin spun Cas about until she faced him. She stared into the turtle-dove brown eyes that had seemed so lovely a few days ago.

Dustin said, "Now—"

And Cas smashed her forehead into his. Dustin dropped like a stone tossed in a river. But Cas paid the price and went down with him. Her brain felt like it was bouncing around in her skull.

Despite the pain, she rolled to her knees. That move worked all the time in the movies. But the hero never looked close to tossing his cookies afterward, like how Cas felt now. Dustin's eyes fluttered, but he wasn't moving. She might not have much time before he woke up. She scooted toward him, but it was slow, painful going.

"Where is it? Where is it?" Cas cried out in a hoarse whisper as she searched around Dustin for the blade. She leaned over his torso and searched the floor until her fingers brushed it.

She didn't know how long it took to cut through the material around her ankles but then it was done. Cas kept a grip on the blade, staggered to her feet, and ran.

Cas darted toward the door. She stumbled once—her feet were numb from being bound for so long. But she made it into the hallway and ran as fast as she could for the reception area. She heard a crash in the council chamber. Dustin was coming.

Once she was through the waiting room and down the hall, she paused for a moment to consider whether she should take the hover pad or find some stairs. She decided on the hover pad. Even though she'd be a sitting duck while riding, it would give her a moment to rest.

As soon as she stepped off the pad onto the marble floor of the Courthouse's lobby, it streaked upward again. Dustin must have called it back. He was right behind her.

Cas raced for the front door. Once outside, she could blend in with the parade revelers. Her head pounded from the outside in, and her vision blurred for a second. She lumbered sideways and crashed into a wall. The blade bounced and slid across the marble floor out of reach. Cas rubbed at her eyes and forced herself to move again. But Dustin was off the hover pad and running full tilt.

Cas ran in a way she never knew was possible. She crashed into the front door and fumbled with the lock. The door yielded and her heart leapt. She was going to make it.

The street outside had emptied out of all but a few devoted parade goers.

"Cas!" Graham waved from about a block away. At first, he appeared happy to see her but then his features clouded.

She turned, preparing to bolt in his direction. But just then, a hand buried itself in her hair and yanked. Then she was falling.

Cas hit the floor hard enough to knock the breath out of her lungs. For the moment, she could only watch as Dustin closed, locked, and then shoved the door's additional bolts into place. He turned and towered over her. His face contorted into a grimace, and he spat onto the floor.

A door opened across the lobby. Two people in dark green robes edged into her view and stood next to Dustin. Hoods hid their faces. Cas couldn't determine if they were heavy or thin or discern any other basic body features.

"You sure took your time," Dustin growled at them. There was no response. "Whatever. Let's get this over with.

The two robed figures moved to stand on either side of Dustin so they formed a rough triangle around Cas. Dustin pulled the perpetuity stone out of his jacket and handed it to one of the others. "Are you positive you won't need a third person to cast the spell?"

Cas heard one of the robed people scoff before snatching the stone and passing it to the other figure. Together, they bowed their heads and began to chant in a low, monotone hum.

Cas tried to sit up, but Dustin pinned her shoulders down to the ground. She fought to stay conscious and struggled to think. She wriggled her body but couldn't move. Then she did the only thing possible. Cas bit Dustin hard on the forearm.

Dustin swore and backhanded Cas hard. For a minute, the edges of her vision went black. It was literally do or die time, and she refused to go out like this.

Someone pounded on the front door of the Courthouse. It shook and rattled. One of the bolts clattered to the floor, and the door parted a fraction and held. Cas heard Graham shouting on the other side.

From the corner of her eye, Cas saw something squeeze through the parted doorway. It darted around the legs of her captors.

Dustin cackled. "Ah, what do we have here? A failed experiment standing up for a freak of nature?"

Echo's hair stood on end, and he looked twice as big as usual. He hissed. "Let her go."

"Why? I'm about to get everything I ever wanted," Dustin said. He stood and planted a foot in the center of Cas' chest. He withdrew the athame blade Cas had dropped.

Echo prepared to leap, but before he could, one of the robed figures lashed out. The cat didn't see it coming in time. The kick caught him in the ribs.

It was enough of a distraction for Dustin to pick Echo up by the scruff. He held the blade over the cat's chest.

"Echo! No! Let him go!" Cas cried out from the floor.

The chanting grew in intensity. "Drain her. Now!" Dustin hollered at his companions as he cast worried glances at the front doors. "Hurry!"

One of the figures held the stone out toward Cas. As he did so, she saw a wisp of pink smoke emanate from her chest. It weaved from side to side like a cobra being called by a snake charmer.

No. This couldn't happen.

"Now be a good girl and just let them finish, Cascade." Dustin gave Echo a shake, but the cat dangled limp.

A WITCH TOO LATE

Cas moved, but Dustin hissed another warning and put the blade to Echo's throat. "Make a move and he'll go first."

The chant was changing, evolving, as if the spell was becoming more complicated with every syllable. And as it did, Cas could feel her essence ebbing away. The pink, ethereal filament still weaved. It stretched to cross the expanse between Cas and the stone.

Cas looked at Dustin. He had won. She was going to die.

Echo's body hung lifeless. Cas didn't know if he was actually gone, but it didn't matter. Soon, they both would be. Both of them innocents caught up in plots based on greed and power lust.

She was innocent. And so was Echo. She levelled a look at Dustin and he...smiled. It was an expression of pure smug satisfaction and glee. He'd won and knew it.

The pain didn't come this time, but the fury did. It exploded up from a place within her that held every buried truth, every rejection, every moment of sheer confusion and doubt and hurt. And most of all, the pure rage of her friend being threatened pushed it all over the top.

The wisp was almost to the rock now.

"Put. Him. Down." Her voice held only a hint of menace.

Dustin laughed.

Cas let the door containing all the hurt burst free. And it did. The magical bindings that attempted to restrain the most powerful part of her being fell away, scorched and smoking.

She didn't have to visualize anything this time. Cas was an all-consuming giant. A powerful being with one intention.

A single word slipped from behind her clenched teeth. "Hot."

Dustin smirked. "Really? Did you think that would work? The spell on you is so strong, nothing could break—"

He didn't finish as his eyes snapped to the arm holding Echo. The fabric of Dustin's jacket smoldered. Swaths of it began to fall away like ash. He dropped the cat just before his screams started.

Cas dove and caught Echo just before his limp body struck the floor.

Dustin's shirt sleeves disintegrated to dust as if being consumed by invisible flames. The skin of his forearm smoked. Frantic, he howled and slapped at it, only to snatch back his hand like it had caught fire too.

The chanting faltered as he screamed. Cas shifted Echo to the crook of one arm and struggled to her feet. As she rose, Dustin dropped. Inhuman sounds escaped his mouth as he made a feeble attempt to crawl away.

The robed figure holding the stone stopped chanting and took a defensive step backward. The other person grabbed at the sleeve of the first one's cloak. "We still need her." But the other one wasn't having it.

The one who had spoken growled in frustration and lifted a hand, performing the first gestures of a spell.

Cas flung up a hand, ready to fight, to defend...

The front door of the Courthouse crashed open. A deafening roar filled the lobby.

Everyone in the room froze.

The threshold of the Courthouse was barely large enough to contain what stood there. A black bear, as wide across the shoulders as three adult men standing side by side, blocked the moonlight coming in from the street.

A WITCH TOO LATE

The bear bellowed, baring curved incisors and dripping spittle. It stopped and moved its head from side to side to take in the scene.

With a cry, the robed figures broke ranks. They sprinted across the lobby, heading for a side door. The bear cast a glance at Cas as it went by. She stared after it, open-mouthed.

Movement in her arms drew Cas' attention. Echo's green-gold eyes peered up. He croaked, "He's a friend. No worries."

Cas stumbled toward Dustin. He lay whimpering on the floor, wisps of smoke rising from his clothes. Areas of his forearm resembled rivulets of melted wax. "How did you do that?" he panted, peering up into her face.

Cas knew she must look like a wild woman. Her clothes were torn, and her hair felt like it was a giant, wavy mass. A half dozen scrapes stung her face and arms. Yet she smiled and was rewarded with a look of fear on Dustin's sooty face.

Cas had never felt so powerful, so alive, or so relieved.

She snorted and sneered at Dustin the way he'd grimaced at her so many times in the last hour. Then she barked out an answer, feeling the powerful satisfaction of it in her bones. "I'm a witch—what did you expect?"

Chapter 16

Cascade wiped her hands on a paint-stained rag. She looked around and smiled, satisfied. Her coral-colored entryway had two coats of paint. It was done, and it looked just the way she'd hoped.

A loud purr caught Cas' attention, and she grinned at Echo. He was lying on his back, kicking and batting at a hanging vine from a spider plant on the entryway's table. "Paint fumes making you frisky, cat?" she asked him, laughing. He purred in response, his eyes half closed.

Cas busied herself tidying up the paint can and brushes in the big washtub in the laundry room. A knock at the front door brought her back out to the entryway. "Don't touch the walls—they're wet," she told Graham as she gestured for him to come in.

They made their way to the living room, and Cas noticed he had one hand behind him. "What do you have back there?" she asked, sticking her neck out to try and see.

He laughed and whipped his hand around. It held a white-frosted cupcake with a single candle protruding from its top. "Happy birthday," he said.

Cas clapped her hands like a child. "Ooh! A cupcake—my favorite," she said. "Thank you." She cocked her head and examined his face. "Your chin is bruised," she said.

Graham set the cupcake on the table and touched his chin. "Yeah. I guess I ran into something."

Cas pursed her lips and smirked. Two days had passed since her altercation with Dustin in the Courthouse. Graham had jogged into the lobby right after a peacekeeper squad showed up, cuffed Dustin, and took him away. Her gorgeous neighbor brought her home later, and this was the first time she'd seen him since then.

Cas made some tea while they chatted. Echo got tired of playing with the plant and curled up on a chair in the living room for a nap.

"Have you heard anything about Dustin?" Cas asked. She set two cups of tea on the table and sat down across from Graham.

He grinned. "He's real busted up. You did a number on him, for sure. The Council plans to punish him pretty severely, but they're backlogged right now. Lots of mischief cases for them to make their way through, between the ADSB conference and Founder's Day shenanigans. Plus, they're short an Archsiren, and they'll have to gear up for a sit-in to appoint a new one within the next thirty days." At Cas' questioning look, he explained, "It's sort of like a conclave to choose a new pope. Plus, they're still hoping to track down Dustin's robed companions so they can bring them all to justice." He paused for a drink of tea. "So he's sitting in a cell, bandaged from top to bottom, thinking about what life is like at Sitegard."

Cas tilted her head. "Well, I hope justice is served. I feel kind of bad for Dustin, but he went off the rails, and he's a danger now."

A knock sounded at the front door. Cas opened it to find Mr. Percy standing there, staring at the ground. He looked gaunt and a little ill. Cas was silent as she waited for him to explain why he was there. She felt Graham come up behind her. Percy glanced up at him and then back down again.

"I came to tell you that the Council has contacted me and let me know they'll be hearing my case in a few months. In the meantime, they levied some fines."

"Okay. Thanks for letting me know," Cas said. She started to close the door.

Percy leaned forward and spoke quickly. "I was thinking about things, and I would really like the chance to try and make some amends."

Cas shook her head. "I don't see how . . ." she began.

"I have an idea about it." Percy shifted his feet and stuffed his hands in his pockets. "Um, you're still really strong, right? Magically, I mean. And dampening bindings help some, but they're so restrictive that you can't really practice controlling your magic at all while they're in place. . ."

He paused for her reaction, so she nodded.

"I can help," he said. "I can siphon a bit of your energy off every day—no, no, just enough to keep you from being dangerous!" He spoke faster as Cas shook her head. "It will be painless, and because of your abundance now, it won't even make you feel tired anymore."

Cas glanced over her shoulder at Graham and raised an eyebrow. He shrugged in return. "It sounds like it could work," he said.

"I'm in a lot of trouble for having possession of a forbidden magical item," Percy said. "I can't go out of town, and I need to stay far away from trouble. I'm not going to do anything other than try to help with controlling your power."

Cas was quiet for a moment. The peacekeeper squad at the Courthouse had tried to patch Tempeste's bindings, but they weren't strong. She'd caused a small rainstorm in the laundry room the day before. "I'll give it some thought, Mr. Percy. I'll let you know." The incubus nodded and retreated off the porch.

She watched him go. Some neighborhood kids raced by on their bikes while screaming with laughter. Their glee was contagious, and it made Cas grin despite the unease she'd felt after Percy's suggestion. Then she noticed a woman strolling down the sidewalk on the other side of the street.

The woman walked with a skip in her step. And though Cas couldn't hear it, the woman's mouth moved as if she whistled. When she was opposite Cas' house, the woman turned.

Cas waited a beat and then waved.

Violaine waved back. Then she continued on her way, whistling.

Much to Cas' relief, she didn't go—*poof*—and disappear. Instead, Violaine sauntered to the end of the block and rounded the corner.

"Speaking of controlling your power," Graham said after Cas closed the door. "Siren Shiloh told me the Council will deliberate about who might be able help you learn magic. They're making that issue a priority. I told them what you said about Violette offering to help, and they'll take that under consideration."

"Thank you. I also want to talk with them about assigning someone to help Aunt Petunia. I think she needs someone to look after her."

Graham nodded.

Cas felt a small smile playing on her lips. "And I want to ask them about something I saw the other day," she said.

Graham's eyebrows shot up. "Oh really? What's that?"

"Well, I suffered a big bump on the head, but the peacekeeper medics said it wasn't a concussion, so I don't think I was seeing things." Cas feigned puzzlement.

Graham chuckled. "Yes?"

"I could have sworn I heard you banging on the door to the Courthouse and shouting while I was in there with Dustin. But when the door crashed open, it was an enormous bear that barreled in, not you."

"Huh. Strange," Graham said, looking at his fingernails and fighting back a smile.

"Yeah. Strange. Gorgeous, though. Very strong and brave." Cas stepped a little closer to Graham. "And masculine."

"Sounds like a shifter I know," he said. "I could probably arrange an introduction."

"How about you arrange a date?" Cas said, unabashed. "I'll take that shifter out for a drink, and he can show me how he keeps all that hair . . . er, fur . . . so soft and manageable." She ran a hand through her own locks, which still needed a trim. "I could use the tips."

Graham's face broke out in a wide smile, and a chuckle started low in his chest and rumbled up into his throat. He nodded. "I think he'd like that. Happy birthday, Cascade."

"Thanks," Cas said. She sneezed, and colorful fireworks erupted above them. She tipped her head back to watch them and laughed. "Life begins at fifty," she said with a happy sigh.

The End

Dear Reader,

If you've enjoyed this book, please leave a review. We would very much appreciate your support.
Thanks!
M.E. and Paula

Free Book

Sign up for Crystal Springs Mystery mailing list and receive
Dead Witch Talking – The Prequel
Crystal Springs Mystery Books[1]
crystalspringsmystery.meharmon.com

---

1. http://crystalspringsmystery.meharmon.com/

Visit M E Harmon's Amazon Author Page:
amazon.com/author/meharmon

About Paula Lester

Sign up for Paula's newsletter to receive information on book releases, other fun information, book recommendations, promos, and more: https://sendfox.com/lp/10q2rm
You can see all of Paula's books at: www.paulalester.com

***

Works by Paula Lester:

***

**Beachside Books Magical Cozy Mysteries
(Co-Authored with Lisa B. Thomas)**
Pasta, Pirates and Poison
Apples, Actors and Axes
Grits, Gamblers and Grudges
Candy, Carpenters and Candlesticks
Meatballs, Mistletoe and Murder
Honey, Hearts and Homicide

***

**Crystal Springs Cozy Witch Mysteries
(Co-Authored with M.E. Harmon)**
Dead Witch Talking (prequel novella)
A Witch Too Late
A Witch Too Hot
A Witch Too Bright
A Witch Too Dead
A Witch Too Frozen
A Witch Too Soon

***

**Isles of Mer Cozy Witch Mysteries
(Co-Authored with M.E. Harmon)**
Sandy Seances
Seaside Spells
Bewitched Breakers

***

**Cruise Ship Cozy Mysteries
(Co-Authored with M.E. Harmon)**
Cruising for a Bruising
Angling for a Strangling
Yearning for a Burning

***

Sunnyside Retired Witches Community Mysteries
Ghostly Trails
A Bottle Full of Djinn
Loony Town
Mummy Issues
Clairvoyant Clues
Boss Blues
Engine Repairs
Wedding Whack
Turnabout Time

***

Sunnyside Magical Bakery Cozy Mysteries
Sugar Skulls and Suspects
Tea Tarts and Trespassers
Mint Macarons and Murderers

***

Superior Bay Witch Doctor Mysteries
Witch Doggone Killer?
The Affairs of Witches
Witch Way Out?

Unfamiliar Magic Mysteries
Infurior Magic

***

Tessa Randolph Grim Reaper Cozy Mysteries (Co-Authored with Christine Zane Thomas)
Grim and Bear It
The Scythe's Secrets
Reap What She Sows

www.ingramcontent.com/pod-product-compliance
Lightning Source LLC
LaVergne TN
LVHW090346010425
807428LV00024B/143